THE THANKSGIVING GANG

BOOK TWO OF THE TIME MAGNET SERIES

RUSSELL F. MORAN

ISBN-10: 0-9895546-4-3
ISBN-13: 978-0-9895546-4-0
Library of Congress Control Number: 2014913054
CreateSpace Independent Publishing Platform
North Charleston, South Carolina

PREFACE

The Thanksgiving Gang is Book Two of the *Time Magnet Series.*
The Gray Ship was Book One.

The Thanksgiving Gang, like the other books in *The Time Magnet* series, is a novel about time travel, a genre that many authors love because it poses the wonderful question—*what if?*

I suppose I should say here that *The Thanksgiving Gang* is a book of fiction, and any resemblance to real characters is coincidental except for historical figures who are identified. But don't think of it as fiction, even though it is just that. Think of it as a journey that I'm inviting you to join. Soon you'll get to know Jack and his old friend Bennie, Ashley, Jack's beautiful Navy captain wife, Wally (he's new, as is Janice).

Some of the characters in this book are radical Islamists, hijackers of one of the world's great religions. Nothing in this book is intended to cast dispersion on the faith of Islam itself, only the radical fundamentalists who have perverted it.

Like many an author, I felt a relationship with the characters I created in my first book in the series, *The Gray Ship.* I wanted to see what they would do in the future, how they would respond to new challenges, and how they would handle the weird situations I put them in. Part of the joy of writing a series is that I get to continue enjoying the characters and share this joy with my loyal readers, who, after all, are what a book is all about.

I've done a couple of different things in this book. First, I've added a **list of characters**. I don't know why all novelists don't do this. If you meet a character on page five, and then encounter her again on page ninety-five, you've probably forgotten who she is. Bookmark that page and use it to enhance your enjoyment of the book.

Second, I've put in a **time line**. Time travel can be dizzying as one goes back and forth through the dimension, especially if, like Jack Thurber, you go into the future and skip over a life-changing event.

So join me, Jack, and the gang as we step, once again, on a wormhole.

DEDICATION

To Lynda, my wife, collaborator, and editor. We've travelled through time together, forty-five-years and counting.

Characters in *The Thanksgiving Gang*

Abboud, Ayham - al Qaeda official and mentor to The Atomic Five

Akhbar, Gamal - CIA agent, aka Buster

Basara, Hussein - al Qaeda operative in Denver

Bellamy, Paul - Head of the New York FBI Joint Terrorism Task Force

Bettenhurst, Jerome, Admiral - Chief of Naval Intelligence

Blake, Oliver - Deputy to CIA Director Bill Carlini

Bollinger, Ike - Captain, *USS Carl Vinson*

Boulos, Amjad - Sheik Ayham Abboud's driver and assistant

Burton, Wallace - Reporter, *The New York Times*

Buster - CIA agent, aka Gamal Akhbar

Carlini, Bill - CIA Director

Carter, Richard - former XO of the *USS Abraham Lincoln*

Cooper, Jerry - Deputy to Paul Bellamy of JTTF

Cummings, Mike - current XO of the *USS Abraham Lincoln*

Guarino, Sal - Construction foreman at the wormhole site

Haddad, Abbas - Senior al Qaeda official

Hakimi, Ali - al Qaeda operative in Detroit

Martin, Ralph - Weapons Officer, *USS Carl Vinson*

McMartin, Trevor - Australian bank examiner, aka Yousef Salem

Monahan, Janice - Wife of LCDR Joseph Monahan

Monahan, Joseph, LCDR - Weapons Officer, *USS Abraham Lincoln*

Murphy, Philip, LCDR - Weapons Officer, *USS George Washington*

Patterson, Ashley - Captain, *USS Abraham Lincoln*

Peyton, Frederick, LCDR - Weapons Officer, *USS Theodore Roosevelt*

Quentin, George - Weapons Officer, *USS Harry S. Truman*

Riordan, Seamus - See Benjamin Weinberg

Sampson, Father Rick - Priest and friend of Ashley and Jack

Sharif - waiter/CIA operative, Hotel Al Saeed

Thompson, Frank - Rear Admiral, United States Navy

Thurber, Jack - *The Time Magnet*

Trushenko, Vladimir - Russian bomb expert.

Watson, Sarah - FBI Director

Weinberg, Benjamin - NYPD Psychiatrist

Yousef, Salem - aka Trevor McMartin

Time Line - *The Thanksgiving Gang*

May 17, 2014 - Jack and Ashley are married

August, 2014 - Ashley takes command of the *Abraham Lincoln*

July 1, 2015 - Jack slips through the wormhole

July 1, 2017 - The other side of the wormhole

October 1, 2015 - Jack returns to 2015

October 16, 2015 - Operation Tango Delta

November 26, 2015 - The Thanksgiving Attacks

CHAPTER 1

It happened again.

I didn't see it coming.

I never do.

My name is Jack Thurber, and I'm a time traveler, not a title I thought I'd aspire to, but having done it three times before, I guess it's who I am.

I slipped through wormholes before, once travelling back to the 1920s, once to Pearl Harbor in 1941 while it was being attacked, and once to the Civil War. This is getting old.

But this time it's different. I've tripped into the future, two years to be exact. Moments ago it was 9 AM on July 1, 2015. Now, according to a news ticker on a building, it's July 1, 2017. I had been walking through an abandoned lot on the upper East Side of Manhattan doing research for a feature magazine article for the *Washington Times* on underutilized real estate, when I stepped on a storm grate. I felt dizzy, a little nauseated as I always do. Think of the feeling you have when you get off a roller coaster. The scenery didn't change much. The lot was still abandoned but it had sprouted two more years-worth of weeds. It was pouring rain. In 2015, a few moments before, it had been a bright day without a cloud in the sky. It's a strange feeling to step on a metal grate and go from sunshine to rain in an instant. The gloomy weather wasn't helping my mood.

I've got the drill down by now. The grate was a wormhole, also known as a time portal. Step on it and you're in for a weird trip. Your world changes fast, very fast. Here's what I've learned: When you step through a wormhole, the way to go back is to find the wormhole and just step on it again. So right now I can simply step on the grate and go backwards two years. But I'm an investigative journalist. How can I pass up a story, even one that I may never tell? Could *you* resist the urge to know what happened in the past two years?

My first impulse was to go to my New York apartment. I didn't have too much cash on me so I took the subway. As the train clacked along the tracks I stared at an ad for a Broadway play that I never heard of. At the other end of the car, a kid was playing a song on a boom box, a song I'd never heard.

When I got to my condo on East 66th Street, my world became even stranger. The block looked the same as the last time I was there. The brownstone building looks beautiful as always. It cost me a fortune when I bought it a few years ago but I have the money. My book royalties and my job kick off a nice income. My key didn't work, so I rang the bell. With any luck, Mrs. Carlucci the cleaning lady would be there. I noticed that the wooden door had been freshly stained. A tall guy, maybe 60 years old, answered the door and asked me what I wanted. I blurted out a simple truth, at least it was simple to me.

"I live here," I said.

He asked my name. When I told him he said, "Of course, Jack Thurber, the famous writer. I bought this place from a trust in your name about a year ago. The attorneys handled the closing."

The guy looked nervous, even frightened. Can you blame him? I stood there, wet and disheveled, telling him that I live in his apartment. I didn't think it a good idea to tell him that I time tripped from 2015, so I just apologized and said that I must be confused. Time travelers have to choose their conversations carefully.

I was tempted to go to a library and Google myself to see what I've been up to for the past two years, but a knot formed in my stomach, a sudden fear that I may see something I didn't want to see. Time travel has that effect on me.

The rain had stopped so I didn't need shelter to make a call. I took out my phone to call my wife Ashley, but I stopped. There's no one in the world I like to talk to more than Ashley, but I didn't want to upset her. A Navy captain, she had just taken command of the aircraft carrier *USS Abraham Lincoln*, and they're putting to sea today (today?) for a two-week training cruise. I knew she had her hands full. Also, she hadn't *just* taken command, that was in 2014. Then the thought occurred to me: how can I make a phone call two-years into the past? Time travel plays strange tricks with your head.

Bennie, of course! Dr. Benjamin Weinberg is a psychiatrist with the New York City Police Department and my best friend. He collaborated with me on a book I wrote about, what else, time travel. Bennie's popular with prosecutors for his ability to detect lies from people on a witness stand. He vetted some of the people I interviewed for my book, *Living History – Stories of Time Travel Through the Ages*. He also saved my life, pulling me back from the brink of suicide over the death of my first wife, Nancy, in a horrible car accident.

I called Bennie's number, but the phone showed a message, "Your account is no longer in service. To set up a new account please call Verizon or visit our website."

Why the hell would I cancel a phone number that I've had for years, I wondered. Then I realized that Verizon hadn't heard from me in two years, so I walked into a store and paid cash for a cell phone with pre-purchased minutes.

"Bennie, it's Jack, Jack Thurber," I said when he picked up the phone.

"Who the fuck are you, Buddy?" Besides being a shrink, Bennie is also a cop, and his language tends to be blunt.

"It's Jack Thurber, Ben, do you want me to spell it? I'm four blocks from your office. Can I come to see you?"

When I entered Bennie's office on 61st Street, he was standing there with a Glock in his hand.

"Nice way to greet an old friend," I said.

Bennie's face turned pasty white. He put his gun on his desk and plumped down into his chair.

"Ben, are you okay"

"No, I'm not."

"What's the matter?"

"You're dead, my friend. You died almost two years ago."

CHAPTER 2

Bennie was sweating like a cold beer barrel on a hot summer day. He stared at me without saying anything. I saw a roll of paper towels in the corner by a wet bar. I walked over to the bar and I handed the roll to Bennie, who tore off a few sheets and wiped the sweat from his face.

Somebody had to talk first, and Ben wasn't up to the task.

"I've done it again, Ben. I time traveled, this time into the future. I came here from July 1, 2015.

Ben stared at me and didn't say anything. Then he started to cry. Ben would always tell people not to bottle up their emotions, and he was taking his own advice. He couldn't get any words out through the sobs. When the sobbing stopped, he wiped his eyes with and blew his nose.

"Bennie, I think you owe your old friend an explanation." My heart was pounding like a kettledrum. Bennie's crying fit told me that the explanation wouldn't be a happy one.

"It was November 26, 2015, Thanksgiving Day," said Ben. "You and a bunch of other civilians were aboard the *Abraham Lincoln* with Captain Patterson, your beautiful wife, enjoying a special Navy League dinner. The ship was off the coast of New Jersey, steaming for Norfolk, Virginia. According to the news reports, the bomb detonated at exactly three o'clock in the afternoon. It was a nuclear bomb.

Nobody survived, of course, including you." Bennie looked up at me, some fresh tears running down his face. "But here you are, Jack, sitting in my office."

Now it was my turn to be quiet. When a guy tells you that you and your wife are dead, it does nothing for a conversation.

"Come over here and roll up your left sleeve," Bennie said. He looked at my arm. "There's that scar you got from an accident as a kid. It's really you, isn't it Jack?"

I couldn't breathe. I've experienced the weirdness of time travel before, but here is my friend telling me that I no longer exist. Ashley no longer exists. My world is over. Minutes passed before either of us said anything.

"It gets worse, Jack, if that makes any sense. Within five minutes of the first explosion, four more ships were nuked. They were all aircraft carriers, which made these attacks even worse than Pearl Harbor. Besides the *Abraham Lincoln*, the others that got whacked were the *Harry Truman*, the *George Washington*, the *Carl Vinson* and the *Theodore Roosevelt*. Over 26,000 people died. The death toll could have been a lot more, but all of the ships were at sea. Ever since the attacks, all military installations, including ships, have been under lockdown. To get onto a military base or a ship you almost need an Act of Congress. All of the cadets at West Point and the midshipmen at Annapolis now carry side arms wherever they go, including to class. Remember the annual Fleet Week in New York? That's been put on permanent hold. The idea of having a bunch of unidentified civilians sightseeing on ships is out the window. And it's not just military installations that have changed. As you walked here, did you notice more cops than you've seen before?"

"Yes, I thought there must be a police funeral or something," I said. "The streets are crawling with cops. It looks like a different world than the one I left a little while ago."

I changed the subject to a question, the obvious question. "Who did it Ben?"

"A nuclear explosion doesn't leave much of a crime scene to investigate. The FBI, Naval Intelligence and God knows how many other agencies are combing through the personnel records of every sailor in the fleet at that time."

"Anybody claim responsibility? Al Qaeda?"

"Nobody. Not a peep. Not a clue. Everybody guesses that it's al Qaeda, but nobody's stepped up to claim the prize."

"But what's the purpose of a terrorist attack unless somebody brags about it?"

"That's what has the government freaking out, Jack. The guess is that whoever did it is keeping it a secret because they're planning more attacks. They found some big vulnerabilities and are still looking to exploit them."

"Where were you when it happened, Ben?"

"I was walking back to my office after a court appearance. The *Lincoln* blew up off New Jersey about 50 miles from where I stood but I heard the blast." Bennie started crying again. "When I heard it was the ship that you and Ashley were on I almost passed out. Jack, you look great. I cannot fucking believe that I'm talking to you."

"That's two of us, my friend. I've time traveled before, but I can't wrap my head around this one."

"You know, Jack, I've never been able to get this time travel stuff through my brain, but here you are, right in front of me, a dead man telling me he came here from the past."

"After the bombings, Ben, what else has changed? Besides the military lockdowns, what does the country look like?"

"It looks like a basic third world dictatorship, Jack. After 9/11, we all were committed to maintaining our way of life. We weren't going to let a bunch of terrorists control us. We lost the Twin Towers, the Pentagon got hit, and God knows where that other flight was headed. But we were able to move on. Except for the goddam security hassles at airports, we bounced back. Mayor Giuliani got on TV and told us all to go shopping, catch a show, take a walk in the park. In other words, carry on like normal. But five Navy ships gone within minutes? That was a game changer, Jack, that was the dawn of a new day, a dark fucking day. We were used to thinking that military sites were secure, but Thanksgiving Day 2015 changed all that."

"So what else has changed, Ben?"

"Well the first thing the president did was to suspend *habeas corpus*, a pretty basic part of our constitution. He then started acting as if war had been declared, and nobody thought to dispute him. So we have one guy running the country, calling all the shots, and issuing commands off the cuff as Commander in Chief. Obama was succeeded by William Reynolds in January of this year. Reynolds put a rubber stamp on all the executive orders that came from the Thanksgiving Attacks."

"President Reynolds?" I asked, "Back in 2015 I don't remember hearing about a candidate named Reynolds."

"William Reynolds was an obscure State Senator from Nebraska. He gave a great speech at a convention and walked away with the big prize on Election Day 2016. He doesn't seem to enjoy his role as *de facto* dictator, but he has the support of the people by huge poll numbers. Thanksgiving Day 2015 changed everybody's thinking. Nobody seems to give a shit about balancing security against civil liberties. People just want to be secure, and they're willing to shave a lot of liberties to get there. I remember during the cold war there were a lot of Russians who longed for the good old days of Joe Stalin. A prick of a dictator if there ever was one, but people liked the stability he brought to the country. The scumbags who planted those bombs were a tipping point. They changed our country."

"So now what, Ben? Ashley's dead — hell, I'm dead — and America's been plunged into darkness."

"Jack, you're the time travel maven. You tell *me* what's next."

"I'll tell you what's next, and I don't even have to think about it. I know what I have to do, Ben. Nothing's ever been clearer. I've got to go back."

"You gonna change history again, Jack?"

"Do I have a choice?"

CHAPTER 3

"Jack, as long as I've known you, even when we worked on your book, I've been skeptical about this time travel business. I think you've made a believer out of me. Shit, you're dead, if you pardon me for reminding you. We're talking about saving thousands of lives, not to mention yours and Ashley's. We're talking about getting back to some sort of normal life. We're talking about reviving the phrase 'American Democracy.' I remember the philosophical horseshit in your book about never changing history. But sometimes history sucks, Jack. I say let's change it. Let's fucking change it. What can I do to help you pull this off?"

"I have time, Ben, 2015 time that is. I need a few days to learn every possible thing there is to know about the attacks. With all due respect to the FBI and the other agencies, nobody is better at picking the fly shit out of the pepper better than me."

"You can set up shop here, Jack. I have an office down the hall that's empty. It has a computer and Internet access. Also, you can stay at my place on 86th Street. I have plenty of room ever since I got divorced.

"I don't want to impose on you, Ben. I'll get a hotel room."

"Do you think your credit card will be accepted?"

"I didn't think of that. I also don't have very much cash."

"Jack, I still get a nice residual royalty income from your book. Here's a couple of hundred for now."

* * *

"Jack, one thing has my head spinning. These events, including your death, actually occurred, we didn't imagine them. It's history. If you pull this off, will all of the reports about the attacks just go away? Will the ships suddenly appear with all their crews, like it never happened? Do we just ignore all that stuff? I don't get it, Jack."

"Ben, ever since I wrote that book you helped me with, I've been called a time travel expert. How many times have you seen me on TV? I'm sure you remember the time when I was a junior officer and Ashley was the captain of the *USS California*. The entire ship slipped through one big wormhole and wound up in the Civil War and stayed in the year 1861 for four months."

"Remember it? It was the most amazing experience of my life. I'm sure you remember that I was hired by the Naval Board of Inquiry to vet the witnesses, including you. It blew my fucking mind. Ashley testified that the *California* actually engaged in Civil War battles. She said that she did this to avoid a four-year war and save over 600,000 lives. So I sat there listening to this stuff, and I'm thinking, wait a minute. This lady's not talking about the history everybody else seemed to know. Then she talked about meeting with Abraham Lincoln, and I almost passed out. My job, which is why I'm known as "Bennie the Bullshit Detector," is to size up the truthfulness of witnesses, to see if they believe their own stories, not whether *I* believe the stories. So the *California*, also known as *The Gray Ship*, was missing for seven hours in 2013, but all of you people testified that she was gone for four months, gone in the year 1861. My head is still twisted from that Board of Inquiry. Jack, you've been my friend for a long time, and I know you're a straight shooter, but I still have a hard time believing what you and the crew of the *California* believe."

"Bennie, I'm dead, remember? People call me an expert on time travel, but that's nonsense. All I know are my experiences. Maybe there is such a thing as an alternate universe, I don't know. Maybe there are two Jacks, one alive in 2015 and one dead today. And maybe there are two Bennies, the one I'm looking at in 2017, and the one who lives in 2015. But the bottom line for me isn't anything philosophical or theoretical. After I gather the evidence, I'm going back to the wormhole, back to 2015, and save Ashley's life as well as my own and a few thousand sailors."

"So after you disappear, Jack, I'll be left with the recollection of this whacky story."

"Something like that, my friend. It's time for us to get to work."

CHAPTER 4

"I now pronounce you man and wife. You may kiss the bride."

I'll never forget Father Rick Sampson saying those words, presiding over one of the happiest moments in my life. Ashley and I met when she was the captain of the *USS California.* I was a lieutenant in the communications department, promoted by Ashley from the rank of seaman. Long story. As Bennie and I discussed, the *California* spent four months in the Civil War, my biggest time trip to date. It had taken me years to get over the loss of my first wife, Nancy, who died in a terrible car crash that I actually witnessed. Thank God for my friend Bennie Weinberg for getting me through that. Ashley lost her husband Felix, a Marine Major killed by a sniper in Afghanistan. We were two lonely people on a strange journey in a strange time. The only positive thing about the *Gray Ship* incident is that we fell in love. Ashley's a rising star in the Navy. A week before our wedding Ashley got her wings as a Navy pilot, and she'll make admiral soon. She has guts, brains, and ability. She singlehandedly changed the course of the Civil War, a neat trick for a black woman, but that's a long story. She's also drop-dead gorgeous. As powerful a woman as she is, I feel like a love-sick teenager around her. Somebody's out to kill her, and me, and I'm not going to let that happen.

Ashley's folks and mine attended the wedding, as well as my younger brother Harry. Father Rick is our good friend, recently retired from the Navy with the rank of captain. He was the chaplain on the *California* when we took our time trip to the nineteenth-century.

After the *California* found its way back to the twenty first-century, Ashley and I took a 30-day leave at my lake house in North Carolina. A few days into our vacation, we both knew that we'd spend the rest of our lives together.

When I left 2015, Ashley commanded the *USS Abraham Lincoln* and we love the irony of the ship's name, the both of us having met the man himself. Time travel's weird, but it does give you some amazing memories. The thought of Ashley dying is now controlling my life. But I need to park my emotions at the curb and put on my investigative reporter's hat. I've got a case to build, research to do, and I have to move fast.

CHAPTER 5

The *USS Abraham Lincoln* is tied up at its home port in Norfolk. Ashley is having lunch with Father Rick at the Officers' Club. He retired from the Navy and is now the pastor of his own parish not far from Norfolk, St. John's Episcopal Church.

"I'm sorry if I seem distracted Father, but I haven't heard from Jack in two hours."

Father Rick let go with his famous belly laugh.

"Ashley, you two haven't even been married a year and you're worried about being out of touch for a couple of hours? Besides, didn't I see Jack on TV yesterday morning being interviewed on the *Today Show*?"

"Jack's always on TV," said Ashley. "I joke with him that I married a talking head. I know you think I'm just a love-struck newlywed, but my concern isn't dumb. I called him and the message said the number wasn't in service. He's had that phone number forever. I emailed him, and every message got bounced back. I texted him and got the same message as when I called him. I tried his office at the *Washington Times*, and he hasn't been in."

"I wouldn't worry about it, Ashley. A call to tech support will straighten this out. So how do you like being the honcho of a super carrier?" said Father Rick, changing the subject.

"Frankly, Father, the stress is incredible. Compared to being a cruiser skipper, it's like going from small town supervisor to mayor of a big city. As you well know, as my friend and advisor, I've always had this gremlin in me that screams that I'm in over my head, that my career's getting ahead of me. I admit, if only to you, that I'm feeling overwhelmed."

"Then why not look for some post that isn't as heavy duty as running a big warship?"

"Jack and I have talked about just that. I have a friend at the Pentagon who has been dropping hints that I'll make admiral soon. The superintendent's job at the Naval Academy should be opening in a couple of years. I'd love that spot. With Jack at the *Washington Times* and me at Annapolis, we'd work right near each other. Maybe we could actually be like a conventional married couple and enjoy each other's company, without me getting deployed half way around the globe. Maybe we'd even have kids."

"You two make a great couple. When we were on the *California*, I could see that you and Jack had a future together. The most enjoyable wedding ceremony I ever performed was yours."

"Thanks, Father, but the knot in my stomach isn't going away. It reminds me of the first time I flew a jet of the deck of a carrier. If I could just figure out where Jack is."

CHAPTER 6

My name's Dr. Benjamin Weinberg but everybody calls me Bennie. Like a good Jewish boy I made my parents happy by scoring good grades in high school and getting a scholarship to Yale. When I was accepted to Harvard Medical School I thought my mother would float away on her own private cloud.

Mom's joy soon turned sour after I took a strange career turn, well strange to her but perfectly reasonable to me. After doing my residency in psychiatry at NYU Hospital, I joined the New York City Police Department. It wasn't like I walked a beat in a blue uniform swinging a club. I joined the department as a psychiatrist. It seems that I had gained a reputation in an area that warmed the hearts of law enforcement people. I wrote extensively on the subject of evaluating the testimony of witnesses. I studied the field like it was the Rosetta Stone, reading everything I could on the subject and then adding my own papers and books to the literature. I became known as *Bennie the Bullshit Detector* because of my skill at spotting lies. Guys who cheat on their wives feel very uncomfortable around me. Prosecutors love me because I help them win cases. And I love my job because I help to free the good guys and lock up the bad guys. I also find my work fascinating.

My new nickname did nothing for Mom's happiness. She pictured me in a nice Manhattan brownstone, being paid zillions of dollars helping wealthy East Side ladies with their neuroses. I tried to keep my nickname hidden from Mom, but she spotted it on a business card I had made as a joke. Mom was not amused. What saved my relationship with Mom and Dad was the verdict in the *Langston* trial, a notorious murder case that involved some of the biggest stars in Hollywood. After the verdict, yours truly was on every TV news show talking about how I spotted lies and inconsistencies in some of the key witnesses in the trial. So mom was able to email YouTube links to her friends with the subject line reading, "That's my Bennie." Mom can be embarrassing but I love her.

All of which brings me to my strange relationship with my good friend Jack Thurber. Jack's probably the smartest guy I've ever met. He's a big-time journalist and author who loves to dig into areas that others have ignored. He scored a deal from Random House to write a book called *Living History – Stories of Time Travel Through the Ages*. Part of his research was to interview people who claim to have traveled through time. Jack heard about me, having seen me on TV a few times, and called to ask if I'd like to collaborate with him on the book. I figured if there's ever a field of fresh bullshit it's time travel stories. Jack offered me not just a fee but a generous share of his royalties. Besides fun, this was one of the best financial moves I ever made. Today, almost 10 years after the book was published, my royalties checks keep coming. Sharing time with a good friend and making money to boot is a gift from God.

When I interviewed the "time travelers" for the book, my mind was blown. I'm an expert at evaluating psychopaths, people who, among their other traits, can be very good liars. I thought I'd seen them all. Yes, a few of the travelers I interviewed were obvious nut cases (I didn't learn that term at Harvard) but a half dozen were solid as rocks. They said they time travelled and had detailed stories to back them up. Not one of them was lying.

Jack Thurber himself claims to be a "time traveler." I think I mentioned that Jack's a good friend, maybe my best friend, and here's where things got dicey on occasion. Jack would tell me his stories and I determined, professionally, that he wasn't lying a bit, not even stretching the truth. When he was in the Navy about four years ago, he and a ship full of about 630 people claimed to have traveled from the year 2013 back to the Civil War. When the ship "returned" to 2013 the Navy convened a Naval Board of Inquiry to investigate. To help vet the witnesses the Navy hired guess who. It was the second most amazing experience of my life. I'll tell you about the number one amazing experience shortly. Every sailor who took the stand was telling the truth, including Jack and the ship's captain, a beautiful woman who Jack would eventually marry. I told you he was smart.

Okay, for the most amazing experience this bullshit detector ever had, well, I'm still going through it. Jack, along with his lovely wife, were killed two years ago in a terrorist attack on a ship that she commanded. Four other ships were attacked within five minutes. That was in 2015, Thanksgiving Day, to be exact. But here's what's making me nuts. Jack showed up in my office a few days ago, in 2017, very much alive. He wants to travel back through time to 2015 and prevent the attack. I told you it was amazing.

Also, it's no bullshit.

CHAPTER 7

"Bennie, I need you to help me focus on my research. I don't just want to dive in, I want to have some targets to aim at. I want to come up with some stuff that, in retrospect, will look suspicious. I don't want to pounce on people shouting that I just time tripped into the future and found some bad guys. Put your skeptical cop hat on."

"Well, let's start with what we know, Jack, which is very little. A lot has been written about that Army scumbag, Nidal Hassan, who killed 13 and wounded 30 at Fort Hood. There was a lot in his background that should have set off alarms. He never passed up an opportunity to talk about his hatred of America and his love of radical Islam. I'm sure you're going to remind the Navy and the FBI about this case."

"Great points, Bennie. But like you said, Hassan put out a lot of warning flares. People who should have known better just ignored them. How do I tell the folks in 2015 where I got the information on the Thanksgiving Attacks?"

"Jack, the last, the absolute last fucking thing you want to do is to tell them about your little time trip. You're one of the best investigative journalists in the country and nobody's going to doubt that you uncovered the facts. The evidence that we'll be digging up existed before the bombs went off. Also, you have one big advantage over all of the investigators – you'll return to 2015 knowing what will happen in a few months. Pieces of evidence that would otherwise seem insignificant will jump out at you."

Chapter 8

I just came back to Bennie's office from my five-mile run around Central Park and a forty five-minute workout at Planet Fitness, a block away from the office. They're having a 30-day free tryout, so I didn't have to hit up Bennie for money. I like to stay in shape. Good for the brain. It also helps to calm the frantic demons in my stomach. Nobody likes to think about his own death, but I'm surrounded by evidence that I'm already dead.

I'm in the office that Bennie's lending me. It's perfect for concentration, just the right size and equipped with a good PC, Internet access, and a printer. It's airy and has pleasant green and blue walls. Hung on the walls are painting of pastoral scenes from various historical eras. Bennie says that type of art calms him, and I see what he means. The office only has one window that looks at nothing interesting, which is good because if there's one thing that can break a researcher's focus it's a pretty view. If I want to rest my eyes I can look at the paintings. I've decided to start my research by checking the security clearance procedures for all crewmembers at the time of the attacks.

I found that background checks are done through the U.S. Office of Personnel Management (OPM), which uses its own agents as well as private contractors. I came across a *Reuters* article from September 2013 that talks about hundreds of security clearance records that are falsified every year. How nice. OPM has a security clearance budget of about a billion dollars, and part of the bucks go to the private contractors who nobody tracks down. In one case that was prosecuted, an investigator reported that he personally interviewed a guy who had been dead for over 10 years. With that kind of taxpayer dollars sloshing around so many pockets, it's no wonder a lot of people get clearances who shouldn't. Aaron Alexis, the nut who gunned down 13 people at the Washington Navy Yard, had a Secret clearance even though he'd been involved in incidents of violence before and after he got cleared. And then there's Edward Snowden, the contractor for the National Security Agency who divulged a mountain of American and British surveillance documents. His clearance? Top Secret. Both Snowden and the Navy Yard shooter were vetted by USIS, a private company hired by the OPM. And this crap was years before the carriers were nuked. I feel another book coming on. I also feel like I'm gonna puke.

After reading about the screw-ups by the OPM, I have the sinking feeling that there may be no smoking guns, simply because nobody thought to ask the right questions. Oh, Nidal Hassan? Just because he was heard constantly denigrating America and praising radical Islam, and just because he was an Army officer who carried a gun, heck, none of that stuff should cause anybody to put a bad remark into his fitness reports. Okay, I guess I'm just enjoying the smugness you feel when you look at things from hindsight.

Wait a minute. Hold the phone. What's this? According to a *New York Times* article, five officers, all stationed on the nuked ships, had something in common. When each of them was 18 years old, they took a trip to Riyadh, Saudi Arabia, conducted by an organization called *The Center for Open-Minded Youth*. Wallace Burton, the author of the article is an old friend of mine, a classmate at the Columbia School of Journalism. Bless Wally, he doesn't miss a trick. It turns out that *The Center for Open-Minded Youth* specializes in sending American and European kids on special trips to the Middle East for mind stretching. That must take a lot of money, yes? No problem. *The Center for Open-Minded Youth* is funded by Saudi Arabia.

Okay, just because an 18-year-old kid takes a trip to sand land doesn't mean he's a terrorist recruit, but these are five dots, five coincidences, five possible clues. To keep my research focused, I'll call these guys the *Atomic Five*.

I'm thinking about that 1987 movie *No Way Out*, with Kevin Costner playing a naval officer at the Pentagon. He was a deeply imbedded Soviet mole, having been groomed for the job since he was young. Is it possible that the *Atomic Five* have been preparing for their roles since they were kids?

I don't see anything in the research that hints at any radical religious leaning of these officers, just those trips to Saudi Arabia when they were teenagers. According to the personnel records, one of them, Joseph Monahan on Ashley's ship, is listed as an Episcopalian. Then there's Quentin on the *Harry Truman*, who calls himself a Presbyterian, and Martin on the *Carl Vinson*, a Catholic, as is Peyton on the *Theodore Roosevelt*, and Murphy on the *George Washington*. According to Wally's article, the parents of each of these guys told investigators that their sons and their wives were of the same religion as them, except for Peyton who isn't married.

Here's another article by Wally about the names of the officers. He took the angle of searching for stories using the Muslim names of the *Atomic Five*. The article was co-written by Eric Pucinski another great reporter. Eric also reads, writes, and speaks perfect Arabic. That said, this must have been a tough job, because the spelling of Arabic names are notoriously changeable. Not only that, but just because there's an article about Abu Hussein doesn't mean it's the Abu Hussein also known as Joseph Monahan.

So, Wally and Pucinski restricted themselves to stories that include the word American or America or United States. Here's what they found:

Joseph Monahan (Abu Hussein) "...our American brother."

George Quentin (Jazeer Mohammed) "...visiting from his home in the United States."

Ralph Martin (Fatah Zayyaf) "...American brother."

Philip Murphy (Mohammed Islam) "...our American friend."

Nothing much, but here's a bell ringer from a newspaper article in Yemen: "...Lashkar Islamiyah, still uses his infidel name, Frederick Peyton, when he's in America."

Wally also found another "coincidence." Each of these guys was the weapons officer on his ship.

Wow. But why am I thinking *wow*? This is a 2017 *wow*. In 2015 it could be a *so what*. What I mean is that, post attacks, we can connect all sorts of dots. I may conclude that these bastards were Islamist terrorists, but it wouldn't be a cold exercise in logic. We know these facts in 2017 because they're history. But in 2015, before the attacks, the politically correct response to what I've found so far would be, "So, they may be Muslims. Doesn't make them terrorists." Not only politically correct, but accurate. Nothing I've read thus far has any of the blinking red light warnings that Nidal Hassan, the Fort Hood shooter, put out. Numerous post-shooting witnesses testified about Hassan's radical views and diatribes against America. There was none of that from the five officers in question.

I need more. Bennie's right. I can't go back to 2015 and say, "Hi, I just got back from the future and found out that five naval officers are nuclear terrorists."

Bennie dropped into the office to ask me if I wanted some coffee. He asked where I was in my research. I told him about Wally Burton's article in *The New York Times.*

"I haven't found anything that's not already been covered," I said. "I'm going to call my friend Wally Burton from the *Times.* He may be doing follow-up research and I need to compare notes with him."

"Jack, he knows you're dead. Everyone does. How are you going to chat him up when you don't exist?"

"Ben, you make the call. Tell him that you have some information about the attacks. He'll drop everything to see you and when he opens the door, I'll be with you."

"You'll make his day, I'm sure," said Ben.

CHAPTER 9

Wally Burton's secretary escorted us into his office at *The New York Times* Building on Eighth Avenue. Wally's window faced east, giving him a great view of the Empire State Building. Ben introduced himself, and then me, simply as his friend Jack. Wally and I hadn't seen each other for over 15 years. Wally's about six feet and has gained a lot of weight since I last saw him. I recall liking the guy. Smart as a whip with a great sense of humor. Wally has a way of interviewing people that gets straight to the facts, but he it does in a way that puts a person at ease. He's sort of like jay Leno. Friendly and affable, but he always asks the right questions.

Wally stared at me. "You look just like a friend of mine from journalism school named Jack Thurber."

"I *am* Jack Thurber."

It's uncomfortable to tell somebody the impossible. Wally just stared. He didn't say a word. I go through this a lot.

"I guess I owe you an explanation," I said.

"Yes," said Wally, "you do. You're dead."

So I laid it all out for Wally, with Bennie chipping in. Wally, like everyone else in the country, was familiar with the *Gray Ship* incident and my writings on time travel.

"So let me get this straight, Jack. You're not dead, which I can see. You say that you came to us from July 2015, a few months before the Thanksgiving Attacks. I suppose as a reporter I should be excited about this story, but you're freaking me out, my friend, you're totally freaking me out."

"I get it, Wally. I have a hard time believing it myself, but it's the truth. I'm very much alive as you can see, and for me, the attacks didn't happen yet. I have no idea how, but I'm able to travel through time. My wife calls me a time magnet because I seem attracted to time portals or wormholes. You've read about my testimony at the Naval Board of Inquiry in 2013 about the *USS California* incident. I know it sounds impossible, but I'm a time traveler. But now I have one simple objective. I want to get as much evidence as I can and return to 2015 and blow the whistle. I want to save a few thousand lives, including my own and my wife Ashley. And that's why I need your help."

"I'll be happy to help, Jack, not that I can believe any of this. Tell me what I can do."

"I need convincing evidence that the guys you wrote about are potential terrorists. I want to give the authorities in 2015 the ammunition to take action. I need objective data, stuff that will make their hair stand on end. I don't want to tell them that I came from the future and found out that something terrible will soon happen. You dug up some great information, Wally, especially the part about all five of these guys going to a Muslim camp when they were teenagers. But I need more than that. You know as well as I do that a story is never over until the end. And here in 2017, we haven't heard the end of the story yet."

"Yes," Wally said, "I haven't let go of the story, and my recent digging has turned up some new stuff. It's a bitch trying to find sources, but I'm on a trail. Like you, I prefer to interview witnesses. But they're all dead."

"The bad guys are dead, Wally, along with the people they murdered. But there are spouses, kids, parents, siblings. We can interview them on the ruse that we're doing a story on the families of those who were killed in the Thanksgiving Attacks. It's been two years, so emotions won't be too raw. We'll just be asking them questions about their departed loved ones."

We both turned to look at Bennie.

"Ben, my friend, if the world ever needed a bullshit detector it's now," I said. "How would you like to play journalist and interview these people with us?"

"I'm in," said Bennie.

CHAPTER 10

We stood on the front porch of 200 Darvis Circle, Brooklyn, the home of Janice Monahan, widow of Lieutenant Commander Joseph Monahan, weapons officer on the *USS Abraham Lincoln*. The time was 11 AM, a reasonable hour to ring somebody's doorbell. Neither cops nor journalists like to call in advance to schedule an appointment. The person can always try to duck you. Better to just show up. A car was parked in the driveway, so we assumed Mrs. Monahan would be home.

An attractive woman in her mid to late 30s answered the door. She had the usual look of confusion when somebody is confronted by strangers. She had medium length blond hair, wore tight jeans that caressed her athletic butt, and an MIT sweatshirt. A casual observer may think of her as a knock-out.

"Good morning, Mrs. Monahan," said Wally. "We're from *The New York Times*. My name is Wallace Burton and these are my colleagues, Jack Harper (my new alias) and Ben Weinberg. I hope we're not catching you at a bad time."

"What's this all about?" The standard response.

"We're writing a feature article for *The New York Times Magazine* about the families of the victims of the Thanksgiving Attacks. I know this must still be painful for you, but we'd like to ask you some questions if that's okay."

"I didn't think there were any more questions left to ask, but please come in."

She led us down a short hallway and into a spacious den. She offered us coffee and we all said yes. Never refuse coffee. It opens a small but important relationship with the person you're interviewing.

While she went into the kitchen I took in the details of the den. It was a beautiful room, tastefully decorated with leather furniture. There were arrangements of freshly cut flowers. The shelves along the wall were neatly stacked with books arranged by author name. I noticed that there were no pictures of Joseph Monahan, no Navy mementos, and no display of the military decorations that each victim received. Based on the den only, you would never know she had been married. Was she just trying to forget her late husband? People handle grief in different ways.

She returned from the kitchen carrying a tray and asked us to sit around the coffee table. The table was surrounded by architectural stools which fitted perfectly to the table.

"Please call me Janice. I've been interviewed so many times by Naval Intelligence, the FBI, and not to mention dozens of you news folks. Why the renewed interest after two years?"

"Our article will be about the human toll that the attacks have taken on the families of the victims," Wally lied. "It was the most devastating attack ever on American ships, and we're looking to show our readers the aftermath in human terms."

"Did Commander Monahan show any signs of concern before the ship set sail that day?" I asked.

"No." said Janice. "The *Lincoln* was on a short deployment of a few days, so we didn't have our regular bout of 'when will I see you again?'"

"So nothing seemed to be bothering him?" I said.

"Well, now that I think back, one thing struck me as odd. In the months before the attacks he seemed obsessed with getting an air conditioner for the ship's magazine, the place where they store weapons and ammunition. He was concerned about humidity. Like him, I'm an engineer, and I specialize in heating and air conditioning systems. He constantly talked about it, asking me all sorts of questions about this and that air conditioning system. He even asked me to do research on the ideal a/c system for the weapons magazine. He insisted that the machine be of certain dimensions, which made sense. As the ship's weapons officer, he knew his space inside and out. So I came up with what I considered to be the best air conditioner for the job. It was a real bruiser, a Tomlinson Model 2000. The thing is heavy and measures four feet high by three feet wide and three feet deep. He made constant phone calls to arrange for it to be delivered by a certain date."

"When was the date?" I asked, not sure where I was going with the question.

"I remember it was early November, three weeks before the attacks. In retrospect, Joe's air conditioning concerns were wasted. But I'm sure you don't want to write about air conditioners in your article."

"Reporters ask a lot of stupid questions, Janice, but we never know if they're stupid until we do the research and write the article," Wally said.

"Was Commander Monahan a religious man?" I asked.

"Not particularly, but he did have a lot of curiosity about different religions. He was fascinated by Islam, and read a few books on the subject. When I asked him about it he just said he found the stuff interesting."

"Did he ever express any thought that he may want to convert?" Bennie asked.

"Convert? No, he never went further than his reading. We were church-going Episcopalians, and I still am. He just kept insisting that he found Islam fascinating. Hey, I find HVAC systems fascinating so who am I to ask questions." We all laughed.

"Anything else you'd like to tell us, Janice?" I asked.

"Well, this is weird, it just popped into my head. Getting back to the air conditioner. Joe asked me if I could order five units through my consulting firm. 'Are you looking to dehumidify the magazine or turn it into a meat locker?' I remember asking him. He told me he wasn't the only weapons officer concerned about humidity. I asked him if I could bill the Navy for what was looking like a big job. He insisted that each ship would do the ordering individually. I don't know if this helps your human interest story, but it just occurred to me."

We spoke for some time about Joseph Monahan and her life with him. She didn't have any other recollections so we sensed the interview was coming to a close.

"Janice, we thank you for your time," I said. "We may have some follow-up questions down the road. I'll let you know when the article will be coming out."

CHAPTER 11

We piled into Wally's car and started debriefing before he turned on the ignition.

"So, Dr. Bennie, what do you think of our 'witness'?" I asked. "Was she telling us the truth?"

"Guys, if that woman gave me the name of a horse, I'd bet on it. She inhabits a bullshit-free zone. She's also a hottie, in my professional opinion."

"So, let's see what we have. A guy who finds Islam fascinating and is obsessed with air conditioners," I said.

"That's five air conditioners, Jack," Wally said. "One for each of the ships that got nuked? Am I being too speculative to think that the air conditioners could have something to do with the bombs? Janice Monahan is an expert air conditioning engineer, and she thought his obsession was strange. I wonder why she didn't connect the dots when she was interviewed by Naval Intelligence and the FBI? What do you think, Bennie?"

"The more time between a trauma and the present," Bennie said, "the more the mind starts to speculate without interference from the heart. My guess is that when she went through all those interviews, the last thing she thought about was air conditioners or her husband's interest in Islam. Her brain was still on fire with her sudden loss."

"How do we know she didn't discuss this stuff with the investigators?" I asked. "The interview notes are Top Secret, I'm sure. Maybe the Feds are on to something. It's starting to come clear to me that we should contact the FBI and let them in on what we know."

"You mean divulge a source, Jack?" Wally asked.

"Wally, this isn't journalism as we know it. This is life and death, specifically mine."

CHAPTER 12

After my morning run and workout I sat at my desk in Bennie's office with my head pounding. Our interview with Janice Monahan yesterday opened up a whole new line of inquiry. It almost seems like we may know what happened, at least with one officer on the *Lincoln*. I was in the zone, my question zone, the space in my head where I go when I'm looking for answers.

The phone rang, scaring the hell out of me and snapping me back to the present.

"Jack Thur... er...Harper," I answered.

"Jack, this is Janice Monahan. I need to see you."

"Sure, Janice. Wally, Ben, and I can be there this afternoon."

"No, just you. I'll explain when you get here."

* * *

Janice answered the door, wearing a low cut clingy blouse and a miniskirt, and taking my mind on an unintended trip in a wrong direction. She asked me to have a seat.

"Was there something you forgot to tell us?" I asked.

"You're not Jack Harper, you're Jack Thurber and you're supposed to be dead." She reached into a folder and withdrew a full head and shoulders picture of me from *Time Magazine.* It was an article about the Naval Board of Inquiry after the *Gray Ship* incident.

"I also read, as has everyone else in the world, that you married Captain Ashley Patterson after you left the Navy. Every one of the thousands of newspaper stories after the Thanksgiving Attacks mentioned that you were a civilian guest on the *Abraham Lincoln* when it was bombed. You and Captain Patterson were killed along with everyone else. But you're sitting here in front of me. Very few men in this world have eyes as beautiful as yours, pardon me for saying, and that's how I recognized you. After that strange *California* incident you were constantly on TV and in magazines. This isn't somebody else, is it Jack Thurber? Well is it?"

"I can explain." Well, I can try to explain.

I gave Janice a short summary of my time travel experiences, as if she hadn't read about them already. I told her that for some unknown reason, I seem to find myself travelling through time. I reviewed my experience in the Civil War and the *Gray Ship* incident aboard the *California*, a story that most people find unbelievable. As a cop would say, my cover was blown, so I figured I'd invite Janice into the weird world of Jack Thurber the time traveler.

"Yes, Janice, that's me, Jack Thurber. I've come here from the past. I was killed on the *Abraham Lincoln,* from everything I've read or been told, but I'm alive now because you're looking at me, a guy from 2015. So I guess that clears things up, yes?"

"It's possible that you never made the trip on the *Lincoln*, and you've just been hiding out these last couple of years. That's possible, even if you deny it. I need to hold that thought in my head so that my brain doesn't explode. Does that work for you, bright eyes?"

"Okay," I said, "I understand that you think time travel isn't believable. But let me ask you to hold it as a theoretical possibility. Does that work?"

"Look, handsome (I wish to hell she'd stop flirting with me), then explain what this magazine article baloney is all about." She said this as she crossed her legs, her long beautiful legs.

"Here's the simple (simple?) truth, Janice. My objective is to gather evidence and then return to 2015 to save my life as well as my wife and thousands of others killed in the Thanksgiving Attacks. Wally Burton really is a reporter for *The New York Times*. Ben Weinberg is a NYPD cop and a psychiatrist who specializes in detecting lies from witnesses. Bennie said that every word out of your mouth was the truth, or at least *you* believed it to be the truth."

"Well, Jack, I'm glad Bennie gave me a passing grade. By the way, I know all about him and Wally Burton, as well as you. Engineers know how to use Google too, you know. So, good looking, (stop that crap — *please*) how do I fit into all of this?"

"I was hoping that you may have some ideas on that, Janice. When we interviewed you the other day you gave us some huge leads, especially about the air conditioners and your husband's obsession with them, not to mention his interest in Islam. Something tells me that you have some more information to share with me."

She rubbed her pretty face with her hands and uncrossed those lovely legs.

"Frankly, Hon, I do." (*Hon?* What's with this "Hon"?)

"Everything I told you about Joe was true. When I was interviewed nonstop after the attacks, I didn't go into much detail because my mind was in a different place then. What I didn't tell you the other day were my *thoughts* on Joe's behavior, but I will now. I'm starting to feel very comfortable with you, Jack," she said as she smiled and leaned over toward me. (Holy shit. Should I mention that I'm happily married to a woman from the past?).

"Go ahead, Janice. Do you mind if I take notes? It's a reporter thing?"

"Sure, you can even take pictures." With that she swung her arms outward and faked a back stretch, encouraging her beautiful cleavage skyward. Memo to file: I want Bennie and Wally with me on our next interview.

"Just notes will be fine," I said as I looked down on my notebook and splashed a drop of perspiration on my first sentence.

She then kicked off her shoes, stretched her long legs out and put her bare feet on an ottoman.

Think baseball. Yes, that's it, think baseball. Do NOT think creamy white thighs and beautiful tits. Yesterday's game came back to me. *It's two outs, full count. McCann is on second and Teixeira's at bat. Swing and a miss and the sides retire at the bottom of the fourth with the Yankees leaving one man on base. The score is two to one, Boston.*

"You were telling me about your husband's interest in religion," I said.

"Yes, I told you about Joe's fascination with Islam. Well, to quote Jerry Seinfeld, not that there's anything wrong with that. But it started to go beyond a fascination. Obviously I know that you guys are looking to see if there's a connection between the Thanksgiving Attacks and radical Islam. I guess that's a no-brainer."

"Did he do or say anything to make you think he was becoming radicalized?" I asked.

"A few things. I walked into his study once and he was practicing Arabic with an online language course. I flat out asked him why he was studying Arabic and he said it would enhance his naval career to be fluent in another language. Sounded logical enough so I didn't pursue it. Then he began to use Arabic words and phrases all the time. I only felt uncomfortable when I overhead him speaking halting Arabic with someone on the phone. But I let it go, thinking that you need to use a language to learn it."

"Getting back to my question about any signs of radical thoughts or behavior, can you tell me anything about that?" I asked.

"Yes. One time I saw him watching an online video of that radical American guy who I think is also Yemeni. What's his name? Oh, Anwar Al Awlaki. Hateful stuff. Without any prompting from me, Joe turned and said something like, 'Can you believe this guy? He's one nasty dude.' I got the clear impression that he was trying to throw me off with his negative comment on Awlaki. Sort of like surprising somebody watching porn who then tells you he was just looking for some exercises. I found him watching these videos a number of times, mostly in English, then more and more in Arabic.

"Did his relationship with you start to change at all?"

"Big time. He began to question the way I dressed, especially if I was going out. I'm an exercise nut and I keep my body in pretty good shape in case you haven't noticed."

Oh my God. Yes, I had noticed. Time for another sip of cold water.

"One time as I was leaving to play tennis with a friend, he wanted to know why I had to wear such a short outfit. He went on and on about how much more attractive were the photos from the 1920s when women wore long skirts. He started to get upset whenever I ventured out in anything like what I'm wearing now." Some more drops of sweat plunged to my notebook.

"So, Janice, it sounds to me like you were having some doubts about Joe."

"Doubts don't quite sum it up, Jack. I was feeling like we were drifting apart, like he wasn't the man I married. Do you mind if I talk about sex, Jack?"

Holy shit. Where's Ben and Wally when I need them?

"Please go ahead. Do you mind if I have some more cold water?"

"The more he delved into Islam, the more he wanted to control my behavior. He tried to convince me to wear clothing that made me look like a nun. Our sex life started to take a negative turn. To be honest with you Jack, and I've never told this to anybody, I started to find him repulsive. Even out conversations became stilted. It's like I was living with a man I once knew, but knew less and less every day."

"Anything else you can think of, Janice?"

"I'm sure I'll think of more incidents. I'll jot down my thoughts to share with you."

I suggested to Janice that I would like to review my notes with Ben and Wally and schedule another appointment as soon as possible. I stood to leave and she stood also.

"Wow, you've got a pretty nice build for a Pulitzer Prize winner, if I don't say."

Get me out of here — *Now*.

"Oh Jack, one last thing."

"Sure, what is it?"

"Joe may be alive."

Chapter 13

I met with Ben and Wally in a diner around the corner from Ben's office. We had agreed that phone calls should be kept to a minimum so we would always meet in person. We found a booth in a corner where we could have a private conversation, sparing the other patrons our time travel discussion. I brought them up to speed on my unscheduled interview with Janice Monahan and the new information that she shared. I filled them in on the details about Joe Monahan's descent into what may be radical Islam, and then I hit them with the thunderbolt. Janice thinks her husband may be alive. I recommended that we need to have another meeting.

Wally suggested that since she opened up so much to me that maybe I should do the follow up alone. "No," I almost shouted. Those legs, those tits, *NO*. I convinced them that we need as many eyes, ears, and brains as we can muster. And a lot of cold water.

* * *

We all agreed that we'd invite Janice to meet with us in Ben's office. It has a huge conference table and, of course, a psychiatrist's couch in case we need to go subconscious diving. Janice showed up at the exact time scheduled, dressed demurely in a business suit, the skirt of which wasn't too short, just short enough. I insisted we have two pitchers of ice water on the table and that the air conditioning be turned down.

"Janice, I've briefed Ben and Wally about our meeting yesterday," I said. "They may have some questions, but for right now I'd like to fast forward to the last thing you told me. You said that Joseph Monahan may be alive. Please explain."

"At about 8 AM on the day of the Thanksgiving Attacks," Janice said, "I got a call from Rich Carter, the Executive Officer of the *Lincoln*. He said that Joe was feeling sick and the medical officer thought he may be getting the flu. Because the ship wasn't leaving on a combat deployment, just a short cruise, the XO and Captain Patterson decided to send Joe home rather than risk him spreading the flu around the ship. So they had a car take him to the nearest hospital. I expected his call at any minute. An hour went by, then two. I called the hospital, but there was no record of a Joseph Monahan being admitted, or even seen in the emergency room. I assumed that the captain just changed her mind. I tried to call the ship, but it had already cast off and was at sea. An hour later the *Lincoln* exploded."

"So there are two possibilities," I said. "One is that for some reason they decided to keep him aboard. The other is that he escaped."

"Janice," Wally said, "assuming the second possibility, that he escaped, do you have any idea at all where he may be?"

"Yemen. It's a guess, but it's the only one I have. As his religious interests deepened he talked constantly about Yemen and how beautiful it was. He showed me pictures online and even talked about us taking a vacation there. I explained that vacationing in a terrorist nest was not my idea of a good time, and we left it at that. Again, it's only a guess, but it's the one country he talked about constantly."

"I'll have one of my guys check the local plane departures that day, "Bennie said. "I'm sure he wouldn't use his real passport, but it's basic police work."

"Does the name Abu Hussein mean anything to you?" I asked.

"Yes, yes," said Janice, "I saw it scribbled all over papers in the house. Who is it?"

"It could be your husband's adopted Arabic name," I said. Janice just stared and muttered something. I could swear her lips spelled out "bastard."

"Janice," said Wally, "do you know any officers from the other ships that were hit?"

"It's possible, but I can't remember. If you have their names, run them by me."

I pulled out the list from my file folder.

"All of these guys held the rank of lieutenant commander," I said. "Each of them was the weapons officer on his ship. I'll also give you what we think may have been their adopted Arabic names. George Quentin (Jazeer Mohammed), *USS Harry S. Truman*, Ralph Martin (Fatah Zayyaf), *USS Carl Vinson,* Frederick Peyton (Lashkar Islamiyah), *USS Theodore Roosevelt*, and Philip Murphy (Mohammed Hussein), *USS George Washington.*"

"My God, "said Janice, "they all had Islamic names, including Joe? How do you know this?"

"My friend Wally here is one hell of a researcher, Janice," I said.

"To get back to Wally's question," Janice said, "no I don't remember any of those names. You're all welcome to scour the hard drive on Joe's computer. I work as a consultant out of my home, so anytime is fine with me. How about tomorrow at noon? Lunch is on me."

"Janice, I can't tell you how much we appreciate all your help, "I said. "We'll see you tomorrow."

"Jack, could I have a word with you?" Janice said.

"We'll see you later at Wally's office, Jack," said Bennie as he and Wally left. I had borrowed Bennie's car to run some errands so they left without me.

Oh great. These two are leaving me alone with Ms. Gorgeous. After Ben and Wally left, Janice sat next to me at the conference table.

"Jack, I have something to tell you. I met your lovely wife at the officer's club one evening a while back. You were off on assignment somewhere. Captain Patterson is one of the most beautiful and charming women I've ever met. It's easy to see how you fell for her and loved her."

"That's 'love' in the present tense, Janice. Remember, I'm from 2015 and I'm very happily married."

Janice leaned over and put her hand under the table. Oh God no, she's got her hand on my knee.

"Jack, I know you've been through a lot of stress. Losing a beautiful woman like Ashley must have torn you apart." She lowered her voice and leaned closer to me. "Jack, honey, you've got to give this up." (*Honey?* Again she calls me Honey.) "You lost the love of your life, but you're still here. You never died. You've got to give up this time travel bullshit and recognize that you are very much alive. Somehow you missed that cruise and you're just trying to force it out of your head. I'm no shrink, but I'd say you're in denial over the whole thing. Ashley died and you're alive and you feel guilty about that. Another thing I've noticed. There's something going on between you and me. I'm a very traditional gal, and the last thing I would ever do would come between a man and his wife. But you're a widower, Jack. Ashley's dead. You're alive. I'm alive."

With that she squeezed my knee. I reached for some water.

"Janice, yes, there is something going on between us, and I call it friendship. I know that this time travel 'bullshit' as you call it is hard to grasp, but you have to know one thing. It's true. Nobody can explain it, but it's happened to me four times. I'm here from the past, and that's where I belong, along with the woman I exchanged wedding vows with. My objective, my sole objective, is to return to that time and prevent the Thanksgiving Day disaster, saving Ashley, myself, and over 26,000 other people. To the extent that I'm alive, it's what I'm living for."

"So pardon my engineer's skepticism, Jack, but let me see if I have this straight. You find this 'wormhole,' take a trip back to 2015, and prevent the attacks. What about the guy I'm sitting next to? What about me, Bennie, Wally, and everybody else? Will I still be married to that treasonous prick? Do we all slip into a different existence, a world that never knew the Thanksgiving Attacks? Will I ever see you again?"

"Janice, the world knows me as the 'time travel expert' because of my book and my experiences, especially *The Gray Ship* incident. But I don't know any more about this stuff than you. I've just experienced it. I did find that history can be changed. Hell, we changed the Civil War on the *USS California*. After spending seven months in 1861, we came back to 2013, but it was a very different 2013. Someday, if I'm successful, I'll wind up in the present, the one we're going through now. You and I probably won't meet, because we'll have no reason to."

"But, Jack, at least I'll be able to look at your gorgeous face on your endless TV appearances. A handsome guy who I never met. This is freaking me out."

As she's telling me this she's rubbing my thigh.

"Well, Hon, I have to run," Janice said. "I have a meeting with an architect in an hour. You have to meet with Ben and Wally too." She continued to stroke my thigh.

Janice stood. I remained seated.

"Well, aren't you going to stand up, Jack?"

"Stand up?" I said. "Sure, standing's a good thing, but sometimes sitting is okay too. Say, did you hear the score of the Yankee game last night? Ever since Derek Jeter retired they're not as good, but I still love the team. I wonder how the Cubs did too."

Janice looked at me with a confused face. Oh God no, she sat back down.

"Why are you talking about the Yankees, Hon?"

"Oh, sometimes it's good to think about baseball."

"So I'll see you tomorrow for lunch, Jack."

"Janice."

"Yes, Jack?"

"Please let go of my knee."

Chapter 14

My name's Wallace Burton, better known as Wally. I'm a reporter with *The New York Times*, a position I love. I think I was cut out for this job, having worked on my first newspaper in elementary school. I continued my budding career in journalism through high school and college, where I was the Editor of the *Dartmouth Review*.

After Dartmouth I was accepted to the Columbia School of Journalism, a lifelong dream. While at Columbia I met a man named Jack Thurber, a really sharp guy who had already written a couple of books.

Jack Thurber is now a name that is imprinted on my brain, a name I will never forget. As I reporter I always prided myself on my left-brained analytical skills. I didn't take anything for the truth unless I had all the facts and drilled down under those facts. Like my new friend Bennie Weinberg, I consider myself a bullshit detector. More about Bennie later.

Jack has messed with the left side of my brain. My sometimes wise-ass analytical and cynical self has met a man who claims he traveled from the past into the present. He claims that he has to get back to the past to prevent a terrible disaster. Can you blame him? He was killed in that disaster. I'm getting a headache, something that often happens to me when things don't make sense.

Jack showed up in my office a few days ago with Bennie Weinberg from the NYPD. It's been about 15 years since I saw Jack. Like most people, I was sickened that Jack was killed in the Thanksgiving Attacks of 2015. But he was in my office, not dead in my office, but very much alive. At first I thought it was a different guy, just a look-alike. Hey, a lot can change in 15 years. But he and Bennie convinced me to suspend my disbelief and accept the possibility that Jack was telling the truth. I agreed, not to buy into this time travel nonsense, but to give it some mental space and let the conversation roll. Jack is interested in the research I did on the Thanksgiving Attacks, research that seems to point some serious fingers at five possible conspirators. He wants to use my research to find enough evidence to go back to 2015 and stop the attacks from happening. This is doing nothing for my headache.

Jack and Bennie are starting to convince me that maybe Jack really did come here from another time. Jack, Ben, a lady named Janice, and myself have formed a group. We call ourselves the *Thanksgiving Gang.* I know I have some Tylenol around here someplace.

Janice is a beautiful woman, striking even. If I weren't gay and in mourning from the loss of my partner, George, she would command my constant attention. She seems very attracted to Jack and that isn't making him happy. He's an old fashioned monogamous guy who is devoted to his wife. But Janice keeps trying to explain to him that his wife was killed in the Thanksgiving Attacks. But if Jack's wife was killed, so was Jack because he was with her. Ouch, there goes my head again.

Working for *The New York Times* is my dream job. Although its reporting can be politically slanted, the *Times* is rightfully known as The Newspaper of Record. No matter what you think about the politics on the editorial page, you have to admit that the *Times* is a serious newspaper. And here I am, one of the senior reporters, working with a guy who says he's a time traveler.

Maybe after this I can write for *Marvel Comics*.

CHAPTER 15

I needed some exercise, so I walked the 20 blocks from Bennie's place to Wally's office in The *New York Times* Building. It was a bright day with low humidity and the walk felt good.

As I crossed 53rd Street, a cop called out to me in a less than friendly tone.

"Hey, buddy, stop right there."

I was about to discover a big difference between 2015 and 2017.

"Let's see your papers."

"My papers?" I felt like an extra in a 1940s war movie.

"Yes, your papers. Let's see 'em. Now,"

I handed him my wallet.

"It says that you live in Norfolk, Virginia. What's your purpose in New York?"

I can't believe he's asking me about my purpose. Something told me to treat it lightly, so I just said, "I'm here to visit an old friend, Dr. Ben Weinberg. I'm staying at his place on East 86th Street."

"What do you do for a living?"

I'm a newspaper reporter with the *Washington Times*."

"Okay, move on."

* * *

I walked into Wally's office on the 20th floor. I couldn't wait to tell them about my "papers" shakedown with the cop. They were both smiling at me.

"You guys happy to see me?"

"We've both been discussing Janice, "said Bennie. "She seems to have the hots for you." They both laughed.

"And I have the hots for my beautiful wife, who I'd like to see real soon if we can get our work done."

I told them about my experience with the cop.

"Yep," said Wally, "ever since the attacks this country has changed. The president issued an executive order requiring everyone to carry identification and to submit to interrogation."

"And you guys question my desire to go back and change history?"

"Remember Jack," said Wally "we're with you. Listen, Bennie has an idea, an important one. Shoot, Ben."

"Simply put," said Bennie, "we need some artillery and some law behind us. We started this newspaper article ruse to get through to Janice and it worked. But we're involved in some very high level national security stuff. Also, you're going to need some police training to prep you for what may happen on the other side of the wormhole. Paul Bellamy, the head of the New York Field Office of the FBI Joint Terrorism Task Force, is a friend of mine. I suggest that we call and meet him ASAP. I think Janice should join us."

"Hold on guys," I said. "Let's not forget about my mission, my only mission. Remember that? The Feds will just want to pump us for information and take off on their own. Do you think getting Jack Thurber back to a wormhole will be on their radar? They'll just want to prevent another attack."

"I know how these guys operate, Jack," said Bennie. "Hell, I've been on loan to the FBI so many times over the years that I'm thinking of asking for a Federal pension. They're good people, especially Paul Bellamy. My hunch is that, with our combined knowledge, he'll want to deputize us all as provisional agents."

"So what do we tell him? That we're working on a newspaper article, and no kidding, we won't file it till we get the word from the FBI?"

"No, Jack. We've got to enroll Paul Bellamy as the latest member of the Jack Thurber Time Travel Trust. You can't bullshit Bellamy, Jack, and that's fine because you're no bullshitter. Look, you've convinced hard-nosed guys like me and Wally that you've tripped through time. I believe that you convinced Janice too, although I think she'd travel with you anywhere. We can only keep this little secret contained just so tight. We need some big boys behind us. Besides, I'm sure the FBI has some stuff that we haven't uncovered, and I think we've got stuff they don't know about, especially Janice's husband."

I looked at Wally. He closed his eyes and nodded.

"Okay, Ben. Let's make the call and get it rolling."

Ben placed the call to Paul Bellamy and explained the bare outline of what we're up to, without the time travel details for now. Bellamy wants to see us tomorrow at 10 AM. Ben then called Janice to tell her that our meeting would be in Bellamy's office. Janice wanted to talk to me, (surprise, surprise) but I signaled a pantomime wave-off to Ben and he told her I had stepped out.

It was 6 PM, and we all agreed that we should get some rest for our meeting tomorrow. It would be a meeting that none of us will ever forget.

CHAPTER 16

The shrill tweet of a boatswain's pipe sounded throughout the ship. "*Abraham Lincoln*, arriving." This is the standard Navy way of announcing a dignitary, including that person's badge of responsibility. For a commanding officer, it was the name of the ship. Ashley always had to stifle a laugh when she was announced as *Abraham Lincoln*.

* * *

At 1430, or 2:30 PM, weapons officer Joseph Monahan entered Ashley's office for a planned meeting.

"How are you this afternoon, Joe? What's on your mind?"

"Captain, I'm concerned about the humidity level in the ship's magazine. With all of the fire power we have stored there I think it's important that we keep the humidity low."

"I didn't know that was a problem, but I see your point. What do you suggest?"

"I've researched air conditioners, Captain, and I think I came up with one that will do the trick. It's the type of unit that doesn't vent to the outside, and we can install it right inside the main door to the magazine."

"But are you concerned about static electricity becoming a problem?" Ashley asked.

"No, Ma'am. We have so many antistatic devices in these spaces it will never be a concern."

"Well, let's do it then. Put in a requisition and get it installed."

"Aye aye, Captain."

Ashley was confused. She didn't come right out and ask Monahan why he was bothering the commanding officer with such a minor subject. Normally, something like this would be passed through the executive officer, who would then bring it up to the captain in his regular daily report. But then, there was something about Monahan that Ashley found a bit strange, nothing she could put her finger on, just an odd feeling.

Monahan immediately put in a requisition through the Supply Department. He noted on the form that he had picked out a specific unit and model, and he would personally arrange for its delivery and installation. The price was only $1,400 so it didn't raise any concerns for the supply officer who reviewed all requisitions. Besides, the Weapons Department usually gets a lot of latitude from the supply people.

* * *

Ashley is having coffee with her friend Ike Bollinger, Captain of the *USS Carl Vinson*, which is in Norfolk taking on supplies. They're in his office on the *Vinson*.

"Congratulations on your first carrier command, Ashley. How are you finding the job?"

"Ike, you've been at this a lot longer than me, so I don't have to tell you it can be nerve wracking. There's a million things to keep on top of, things that can break down or blow up. Sometimes I wish I was just one of the pilots. Flight school was the most exciting thing I've done in the Navy. But shortly after I got my wings, I was given command of the *Lincoln*. I appreciate you meeting with me, Ike. I need all the guidance I can get."

"Ashley, my friend, you know that you can always get in touch and bounce things off me. Anything in particular that's bugging you?"

"Yeah, one weird thing. It's probably nothing, but I just don't understand it. My weapons officer asked to meet with me about putting a self-contained air conditioner in the magazine. He said he was concerned about humidity. I told him to go ahead, but he seems to be solving a problem that doesn't exist. Does it make sense to you?"

"Wow, that *is* strange. My weapons guy approached me last month about the same thing. It seemed logical as hell. You don't want to have humidity around weapons and ammunition. Like you, I just approved it. It's probably just a matter of being overcautious, something I appreciate from a guy in charge of a lot of fire power."

CHAPTER 17

As head of the New York field office of the FBI Joint Terrorism Task Force, Paul Bellamy is a busy man. Bennie warned us not to be surprised at the guy's calm demeanor. I guess that such a high voltage job requires composure when things can erupt into chaos at any moment.

Bellamy's office is located on the West Side of Manhattan at a location I'm not supposed to disclose so I won't.

We met Janice in the lobby at 9:45 AM. She wore a business suit, but something about the way clothes fitted her it could have been a bikini. The lobby was pure Functional Federal. Nowhere on the walls or floor was anything about the JTTF. It could have been a post office. We then began our tour of security check points and metal detectors.

A young Asian woman gave us a cheery hello and opened the door to Bellamy's office. It was large, not for ceremonial purposes but to accommodate hastily called meetings. On one wall hung an enlarged photograph of the Twin Towers on fire. On the opposite wall hung a beautiful photo of the towers when they were still upright. I assumed that this is an ongoing reminder for Bellamy of the purpose of his job. Paul Bellamy, about 45 years old, walked from behind his desk and shook all of our hands, smiling broadly. Bennie, who's often worked with Bellamy, rated a slap on the shoulder. Ben was right, the guy had a sense of calmness about him. His default facial expression was a smile, and when he spoke his speech and mannerisms didn't let you know he was a hardened cop. If you were a movie booking agent looking for an FBI honcho, Bellamy wouldn't get the job.

"So, Bennie, I see that you've acquired some interesting new friends. The little bit of information you told me on the phone yesterday has me intrigued. So what's up?"

Bennie introduced us.

"Jack Thurber here is a famous journalist from the *Washington Times*."

"Ben, excuse me but I thought that Mr. Thurber was aboard the *Lincoln* when it blew up. I hate to be impolite, Mr. Thurber, but I thought you were dead."

"Well, yeah, more about that later, Paul," Bennie said.

"Wally Burton is with *The New York Times*. You probably recognize his name."

"I do," said Bellamy. "You do fine work, Mr. Burton. You'd make a good cop."

"And Janice Monahan is an engineer. She was married to Joseph Monahan, the weapons officer on the *Abraham Lincoln*," Ben said.

"Bennie, my old friend, can you give me an executive overview of what we're meeting about?"

"You asked for it, Paul, and here it is. We've uncovered evidence about the Thanksgiving Attacks and how they may have happened, including the possibility that at least one of the bombers is still alive. Also, Jack Thurber has some thoughts on how to prevent it."

"Ben, what do you mean prevent it? The attacks were almost two years ago."

"Paul, when I told you we were gonna blow your mind, I wasn't kidding."

"I'll let Jack Thurber take over. Do you remember Jack from all of that nonstop coverage of the *Gray Ship* incident in 2013?"

"Of course I do," said Bellamy. "Anybody with the least bit of curiosity would remember it. It was the most amazing story I'd ever heard. I must admit, it has me rethinking my idea that time travel is impossible. Please go on Mr. Thurber, Jack if I may. Please call me Paul."

As Bennie predicted, I then proceeded to blow Paul Bellamy's mind. I gave him a summary of my time travel experiences and then, with Ben, Wally, and Janice contributing, I reviewed what we know about the attacks, including the possibility that Joseph Monahan may have become a terrorist and could still be alive. We also discussed the air conditioners for the weapons departments, and how five of them were ordered, presumably one for each of the targeted ships.

"Paul, I've come here from the past, from the year 2015," I said. "You thought I was dead. I should be dead, but I traveled through time before the attacks. Yes, all reports tell us that Jack Thurber was a civilian guest on the *Abraham Lincoln* to enjoy a Thanksgiving meal with his wife, Captain Ashley Patterson. So everything we know, now in 2017, tells us that I'm dead, Ashley's dead, and so are over 26,000 other people. But I'm very much alive as you can see. My friend Bennie knows me better than anybody. He can tell you it's me, including an identifying scar on my left arm."

Bellamy turned to Bennie and raised his eyebrows.

"It's him, Paul. The fucker's not kidding."

"So Jack, forgetting for the moment my understandable skepticism, why are you here? Do you have information to share so we can prevent another attack?"

"No, Paul. Yes, I want to share information as well as gather a lot more. But my objective, my sole objective, is to find the time portal, or wormhole as we call it, return to 2015 and prevent the attacks. Bottom line. I want to go back and change history."

Bellamy stood and walked over to his window. He had a great view of the Hudson River. I think he wanted to go for a sail, anything to get away from this weirdness. He walked back to his desk and massaged his face with his hands.

"I'm in the business of helping to keep our country safe," said Bellamy, "to stop terrorists from killing us. By definition, my business lives in the future. I want to keep things from happening that haven't happened yet. Now my head feels like it's floating. You tell me you're alive, that you're Jack Thurber, the Pulitzer Prize winner and time travel expert. Our mutual friend Bennie Weinberg agrees with you."

He stroked his face with his hands again. "Before we go any further, I want to show you something."

Bellamy hit a button and a large screen dropped down from the ceiling about 10 feet from a wall. He then accessed a video file on his hard drive and it flashed on the screen. The video was taken by a CNN news crew and uploaded to satellite where it was then downloaded to various news desks. A festive scene unfolded before us with a bunch of people walking up the gangplank of an aircraft carrier. You could see the captain, who everybody knew was Ashley Patterson, climbing the steps in her dress white uniform. Behind her was a tall man in civilian clothes. Bellamy froze the video. There was a close-up shot of me waving to the camera."

"Does anybody recognize that handsome fella?"

"Oh my God, yes," said Janice. (Janice, please chill!)

"You can see the time stamp in the lower right corner of the screen," said Bellamy. "The time is noon, three hours before the ship was destroyed. The next scene is a dining space on the *Lincoln*, showing Captain Patterson, her husband Jack, and other guests about to have Thanksgiving dinner. The scene was shot at sea off the coast of New Jersey at 2:45 PM, 15 minutes before the detonation." He froze the video. "And there is our friend Jack Thurber. But here is the most troubling part of the video. Notice that everybody is still sitting around the table and what looks like mashed potatoes are being served. And there's Jack, enjoying himself. The time is now 3 PM as you can see from the time stamp. Please brace yourselves folks."

There was an ear shattering sound and then, with a sudden rasp, the screen went blank.

"We just witnessed the death of the man sitting in front of me," said Bellamy.

I hadn't seen the video before, obviously. I fought a sudden wave of nausea. Janice burst out crying. Bennie kept shaking his head, saying, "Holy shit."

I turned to Janice. When she stopped crying I said, "No I didn't miss the sailing. I wasn't somehow spared."

"Well folks, I'm a lawyer, trained in logic. What we've just seen tells us that Jack Thurber was killed in the Thanksgiving Attacks. And the only logical explanation for the fact that Jack Thurber is here with us is his story of travelling through time. I hereby file my skepticism in the drawer. You've convinced me that the impossible happened. You've also convinced me that it can be stopped. Jack Thurber wants to change history. God help us. God help us to help him."

CHAPTER 18

"We need to move fast," Bellamy said, "but first there are details. I have to contact Sarah Watson, the FBI Director. I'll suggest to her that I also contact Bill Carlini, the CIA Director. Sarah will clear it with the White House."

"I'm going to recommend to Director Watson that we deputize each of you as provisional FBI agents. That brings up the issue of security clearances. First I need to know, do any of you have a handgun permit? I know Bennie does, of course, and he also has clearance. He's a regular around here. I'll start with Jack."

"Yes," I said, "I have a gun permit, and as a recent naval officer in a ship's communications department I had a pretty high clearance, Top Secret I think."

"Wally?"

"I have a concealed carry permit," Wally said, "and I went through a security clearance check recently for an article I wrote about the Army."

"Great. That leaves you Janice," Said Bellamy.

"Yes, I have a pistol permit," said Janice. "After the attacks personal safety became an issue with me. I'm also an expert marksman, if that's important. As far as security clearances, as recently as three years ago I was lead consultant on a new HVAC system for the Pentagon. I held a Top Secret clearance."

Ben, Wally, and I just stared at Janice. This lady is no slouch, I thought.

"Excellent," said Bellamy. "I'm going to fast track your clearances. From what you've told me I don't think we'll have a problem. Shortly, each of you will become deputy FBI agents. I want to be straight with you folks. This mission could be dangerous. We're looking for evidence of mass murder, and possibly for the murderers themselves. My conversations with Director Watson and Director Carlini of the CIA will be frank and thorough. They need to know Jack's intentions. For that they need to be instructed on time travel, so obviously Jack Thurber will have to be with me when I meet them."

* * *

"We also need to get clear on Jack's cover," Bellamy said. "Jack, after your involvement in that *Gray Ship* incident, your face was plastered all over newspapers, magazines, and TV screens worldwide. It's inevitable that someone will recognize you. So you won't be a journalist named, what was it, Jack Harper? You'll be Jack Thurber. If anyone questions you, thinking you're dead, just say that you missed the sailing and have been away for the last two years. That's a hell of a lot easier than trying to explain time travel. Everybody okay with that?"

We all agreed.

CHAPTER 19

My name is Janice Monahan, a name that I hate. I'll change it back to my maiden name, Kelly, as soon as my lawyer tells me the name-change petition has been granted. The last few days of my life have been strange. Too strange. I've been interviewed once again about the Thanksgiving Attacks of 2015 by three guys posing as reporters from *The New York Times*. Well, one of them actually is with the *Times*.

But one guy I recognized immediately, the famous writer Jack Thurber. I know this sounds stupid, maybe even childish, but I'm falling in love with Jack. How can I fall in love with a guy who I've only met a couple of times? There's something about the man that attracts me like I've never been attracted to anyone before. Any curbstone psychoanalyst will say that I'm just on the rebound from a bad marriage. Bad marriage? What if you found out that your husband murdered thousands of people and then vanished? Yeah, I'd say it was a bad marriage. Some women discover, after the wedding day, that her husband snores, drinks too much, cheats on her, or likes to gamble. But mass murder? That's bad.

Jack Thurber is a wonderful man. Besides his good looks, he's got a way about him that tells you he's the real deal, a man you can trust, a man you can love. I can't stop looking at him. When we separate after a meeting I miss him, I miss him as if he were a soldier who went off to war, even though we'd scheduled another meeting for the next day.

There's one problem, though, a big one. Jack insists he's travelled here from the past and that he was killed along with his wife in the Thanksgiving Attack on the *Abraham Lincoln*. I admit that I've seen some evidence that looked pretty convincing that his story has some truth to it, but I'm still not persuaded. I still think that he must have missed the ship's sailing and that he's here, in the flesh, and not some apparition from another time. I want to help this guy. I want to spend time with him.

I've told Jack that I will help him find that wormhole thingy and go back to 2015 and save the day, but my rational brain tells me that his story is a fantasy made up by a guy who's been traumatized by the death of a beautiful wife.

I'm not a love-struck teenager, but a grown woman, almost 37. I have a math degree from Princeton, an M.S. and a PhD in engineering from MIT. I'm a left-brained empiricist. Show me the facts and I'll put them together for you. I own an engineering consulting company that specializes in heating and air conditioning systems. Sounds boring? I get paid a ton of money for what I do, and I find it fascinating. So here I am contemplating time travel.

Bullshit.

I've read that there's a phenomenon called *survivor's guilt*, common among military people who have lost a friend in combat. It's a psychological burden that a person carries with him when he lost a buddy and somehow managed to survive himself. I think Jack's suffering from this. He knows he should have been on that ship when it was bombed, and he's feeling guilty that his wife is dead and he lived. Somehow, despite a lot of evidence to the contrary, I think that Jack missed the sailing and is beating himself up over it because he lost not just a buddy, but the woman he loved.

Am I being honest with myself, or am I just making up my own story, a story that my heart wants to believe?

I'm not going through an easy time.

CHAPTER 20

We met at the office of Bill Carlini, Director of the CIA. Sarah Watson, Director of the FBI, had been on the job for just a month. Besides Carlini and Watson, also at the meeting were Paul Bellamy of the New York Joint Terrorism Task Force, Wally, Ben, Janice, and myself. The four of us have taken to calling ourselves "The Thanksgiving Gang." The gang sat on one side of the conference table and the Fed honchos on the other.

Turning to the CIA Director, Sarah Watson said, "Bill, I'm going to ask Paul Bellamy to take the lead and bring us up to date."

"Today's meeting will be one you will never forget," said Bellamy. "Rather than explain why, I'm going to ask our journalist friend and provisional FBI Agent Jack Thurber to tell the story of what's happened to date."

After thanking Bellamy, I walked to the head of the conference table, cleared my throat, and told *THE STORY*.

I've noticed that everybody who hears a guy say he's traveled from another time has the same reaction. Sneering disbelief. Can you blame them? No matter how many amazing and tumultuous things happen to us, like 9/11 or the Thanksgiving Attacks, "Tomorrow and tomorrow and tomorrow" as Shakespeare said, "creeps in this petty pace." Directors Watson and Carlini were no different. The only thing that softened their reaction was their respect for Paul Bellamy. Nevertheless, they launched their skeptic rockets.

"I hate to be so blunt in the presence of women, but do you expect us to believe this bullshit?" Carlini said.

"Well, I'm a woman and I second Director Bill's question," Sarah Watson said.

"If I may," said Bellamy, "when these folks were in my office I showed them a video that was made by CNN for its affiliates. It was supposed to be a simple piece of human interest fluff about a bunch of civilians going on a short Navy cruise. The video was never released because the CNN brass thought it would be too upsetting. Bless them, they were right. The public should never see this. I have the video on this flash drive, the video I'm talking about."

He handed the flash drive to Carlini who slipped it into a USB port on his computer.

Bellamy continued, "Now I want to preface this by saying that we've had this clip vetted by the best video experts we have. It's authentic, and hasn't been altered in any way."

Watson lowered a viewing screen and the video played, showing me boarding the *Lincoln* behind Ashley, and then the dramatic scene at the table, the final moment of my life.

The room fell silent for a few awkward minutes.

"When I prepared for this meeting," Carlini said, "I reviewed the findings of the Naval Board of Inquiry after that amazing *Gray Ship* incident in 2013. Jack Thurber here and his colleagues convinced nine hard-nosed Navy admirals that they had travelled through time. That, plus the video we've just seen, tells me that we may have to suspend our disbelief. Your thoughts, Director Watson?"

"Well, for the life of me, I can't imagine why Jack Thurber would want to make this up. But let me address a question to Dr. Weinberg.

Doctor, as a forensic psychiatrist you've done great work for the FBI on the many occasions we borrowed you from the NYPD. You're famous for your ability to assess the truthfulness of a witness. I want to hear it from your mouth. Is Jack Thurber telling the truth?"

"Madam Director," said Bennie, "as I've often reminded people, it's not my job to spot the truth, but to tell if a witness believes it to be the truth. Based on my experience, you can take Jack Thurber's words and inscribe them in stone. He's not lying."

"Okay," said Carlini, "let me see if I can put all this together into an executive summary, which Director Watson and I will soon have to give to the president. Jack, you died in the Thanksgiving Attacks two years ago. Somehow, prior to the attacks, you slipped through a time portal and wound up here in 2017. You've done a lot of digging, with the help of your colleagues here, and you're convinced that you can go back in time and prevent the Thanksgiving Attacks. Would you say that about sums it up?"

"That's pretty close, Mr. Director," I said. "but before I go back I need to have solid evidence that the attacks were being planned. Right now, we think that air conditioners may have been involved and we think the weapons officers on each of the ships were possible conspirators. But right now it's still a theory. I can't go back to the past and say, 'trust me.'"

"Got it, Jack," Said Carlini, "I believe I speak for both myself and Director Watson, that we're prepared to help you in any way we can. I look at it this way — at the very least your work will help prevent a future attack."

"From now on," Carlini continued, "besides your provisional appointments as FBI agents you are also provisional agents of the Central Intelligence Agency."

"Bill, are we ready for our guest?" said Watson.

"I think we are, Sarah. Why don't we show our guest in."

* * *

A woman wearing a burqa entered the room, her robe swaying as she walked. She began to take off her wraps, revealing a man's business suit underneath. When she took of her head garment, she was no woman. A swarthy, handsome man with a full beard stood before us. He stood about six feet tall with a muscular build.

"Folks," Carlini said, "I would like you to meet CIA agent Gamal Akhbar."

"You look lovely this morning, Gamal," said Carlini.

"I don't get paid enough for this abuse, Mr. Director," said Agent Akhbar in a distinctly Brooklyn accent.

The room burst into laughter.

"I should mention that Agent Akhbar has a wise-ass sense of humor," said Carlini, who then introduced Agent Akhbar to each of us. "Agent Akhbar is one of the most valuable operatives in the CIA. He's discovered countless attack plans both on American soil and in other countries. Agent Akhbar is used to operating under deep cover. His name, and even his appearance, change from time to time. Gamal is a Coptic Christian, born in Lebanon, and speaks fluent Arabic. He graduated from American University and has a law degree from Georgetown. He's also handy with a weapon. Once a year we have shooting competitions at the gun range. Agent Akhbar always comes in first. Please say a few words Gamal."

"Good morning," said Gamal Akhbar. "I'm a jihadi's worst nightmare. I look like them, I sound like them, but I'm not one of them. My job with the Agency, as well as my mission in life, is to stop them in their tracks."

"Folks," said Carlini, "part of your assignment will be to travel to various places in the Middle East. Agent Akhbar will be part of your team, although he won't appear to be. Actually Gamal will be in charge of the operation and you will answer directly to him. Besides Gamal, I will assign a team of agents to be there with you. That said, your mission will be dangerous. I think I know Jack Thurber's answer, but I'm going to ask each of you right now, are you willing to be part of this mission?"

"Dr. Ben?"

"I'm in."

"Wally Burton?"

"I told Jack I'm with him. Count on me."

"Janice Monahan?"

"I wouldn't miss it for the world." (and I get to hang around Jack).

I walked over to Agent Akhbar and offered my hand.

"Welcome to the Thanksgiving Gang, Gamal." I said.

Gamal gave me a firm handshake, looked into my eyes and said, "Let's give the American people something to be thankful for, Jack."

"Agent Akhbar knew in advance that he may be working on a mission involving the Thanksgiving Attacks," said Carlini. "What he doesn't know is the full story of how you came to be here, Jack, or where you came from. Give him the full explanation at your meeting with him after this one. It's 1 PM. I'll have lunch served so you folks can get to work in the conference room."

Great. Yet another round of time travel stories followed by the usual, "are you nuts," or "you expect me to believe this shit?" But I'm getting good at this. Besides, Agent Akhbar seems like an easy guy to talk to.

* * *

I decided to wait until we finished lunch before I introduced Gamal to the wonders of time travel. I hate having coleslaw spit at me. As I unfolded my time travel story I thought Gamal was going to bolt for the elevator. I suggested that he call Director Carlini, which he did. The fact that the CIA Director was now a believer seemed to calm him down.

After our plates were cleared we got down to the weird details of what our lives would look like in the near future. We all called our new agent friend by his first name Gamal rather than Agent Akhbar.

"Call me Buster," Gamal said.

"Buster?" we all blurted out.

"Yeah, Buster, like Buster Keaton or Buster Brown."

"How'd you get a nickname like Buster?" I asked.

"Piss me off and you'll find out."

We showed Buster the list of names of the suspected engineering officers, along with their Arabic names. Buster went to a computer terminal and accessed the hard drive in his office two floors below us. He pounded on the keyboard and jotted down notes, punctuated by "holy shit," "fuckin *A,*" and various other colloquialisms.

"To the casual observer," Bennie said to Buster, "it appears that you're connecting a few dots."

"A few dots?" Buster said. "I have each of these names and their possible locations."

"Possible locations?" said Janice. "Where do you place Joseph Monahan, aka Abu Hussein?"

"Yemen," said Buster. "From your reaction, Janice you seem to have guessed that."

"He loves the place," said Janice.

"I guess it's nice if you like dirt, dust, and gunfire," said Buster.

"Buster, you said something about possible locations of the others," I said. "The only indication of a possible survivor is from Janice when she told us that Monahan got sick and left the ship before it sailed. Are you saying they may have all survived?"

"It's possible," said Buster. "I got all this data from our operatives across the Middle East. These are leads. We'll know if they're hot leads once we hit the road. By the way, you reporter types aren't the only ones who know how to sift through data."

"Today's Tuesday. I'd like to fly to our first stop this Friday. We'll travel in three groups. I'm a group of one, and the rest of you will fly in pairs. I'll get our travel people to book us. Our first destination will be Sanaa, Yemen. Janice's husband is the warmest lead we've got so that will be our first stop. Janice, you need to get a black wig. I'll set you up with our clandestine operations office downstairs. If you don't mind me saying so, Janice, you're a very attractive woman. The clan-ops people will fix that. By the time they're done with you, you'll be ready to pose for the centerfold of *Jihad Monthly*. Also, if Joseph Monahan really is there I don't want him spotting you on the street."

"Seamus Riordan, my friend, you good to go?" Buster asked Bennie.

"Seamus Riordan?" the three of us shouted.

"Ah sure, I've got me Irish passport ready to go," said Bennie with a passable Irish brogue. "Long ago the FBI guys realized that Benjamin Weinberg is not a name of choice for Middle East assignments. Fortunately, my mother was born in Ireland, so getting an Emerald Isle passport was easy."

"Okay," said Buster, "a few things I want you guys to drill into your heads in the next few days. First, each of you will have a secure cell phone. We'll communicate with each other using codes, which

I'll give you in a few minutes. You need to memorize the codes, not write them down on the back of your hand, but memorize them. Two, if you see me, you don't know me. We are never to be seen together."

"Will you be wearing your burqa?" Wally asked.

"Very funny, wise-ass. You haven't seen the half of my disguises."

"Three, and this is important," said Buster, "all of you will hit the firing range tomorrow morning at 8 AM. You'll be given your weapons when we arrive in Yemen, but I want you to be up to speed on how to use them."

"Is that really necessary?" asked Janice.

"I hope not," said Buster, "but if you have to use your pistol I want you to hit more than sand."

"What do we want to accomplish in Yemen, Buster?" I asked.

"If possible we want to ID Monahan. Once we do, our operatives will find out everything they can about him. They'll place a GPS device on him and one where he lives."

"How the hell can you plant a GPS on a guy without his knowledge?" asked Wally.

"That's beyond Top Secret and beyond your need to know, my friend. Don't worry about it. We're gonna leash this dog and he won't even know it."

"Okay, it's 5:45. Go back to your hotel, work on your codes, have some dinner, and get a good night's sleep. See you all tomorrow on the firing range."

CHAPTER 21

My name is George Quentin but my Muslim brothers call me Jazeer Mohammed. I'm an American naval officer and the weapons officer of the *USS Harry S. Truman,* a ship that I will destroy in a few weeks, along with about 5,000 heathens.

I suppose that sounds harsh, but it's really a statement of my love and devotion to Allah. It isn't so much that I hate the infidels, as much as it is my desire to do justice for their sinful ways, ways that I know so well. When I was a teenager I would best be described as a juvenile delinquent. I was always in trouble. My grades were terrible, I took drugs and enjoyed sex with the heathen girls. It looked like I was heading toward a failed life.

That all changed in 1994 when I took a school trip that reinvented my life. The trip was to Riyadh, Saudi Arabia and was sponsored by an organization called *The Center for Open-Minded Youth.* Well, open minds it did. I became good friends with four other guys from different parts of the country, Joe Monahan, Ralph Martin, Phil Murphy, and Fred Peyton. The man in charge of us during our stay was Sheik Ayham Abboud, the most important man in my life, my father included, even though the Sheik was just a few years older than me. The old phrase, "a whack upside the head," doesn't do justice to Sheik Abboud's impact on us, especially me. He taught us discipline, dedication, courage, and especially love for Allah and devotion to him and the holy words of the Prophet Muhammad. I was never a religious kid (few delinquents are), but the Sheik opened up a new world to me, a new reality, a new way of processing things. After a month, Sheik Abboud's teachings enveloped us. We all converted to Islam, and swore allegiance to its truth. Transformation is an overused word, but that's exactly what we American teenagers went through. We were new people.

I know it sounds crazy that a troubled youth can straighten himself out overnight, but that's exactly what I did. My parents were amazed. My grades improved, I stopped smoking and sneaking drinks, and I did chores around the house. I also studied and began to memorize the Quran, but never in front of my parents. My sudden upswing in grades got me accepted to Penn State, and also into the NROTC program for training to be a naval officer, as Sheik Abboud counseled.

But Sheik Abboud taught us more than the true faith and how to follow it. He taught us that we were exceptional, that we had a special mission in life, a mission that wouldn't begin for many years. We would meet with him regularly over the years, always focusing on and preparing for our great jihad.

Together, we became the fist of Allah, the vehicles of his justice. Together we will bring America to its knees.

CHAPTER 22

We all had a light breakfast at the hotel and reported to the firing range at Langley at 8 AM as planned. Buster was waiting for us.

"I know you guys have been through this before," said Buster, "but let's review a few procedures. Your weapons are waiting for you in your assigned spaces. Make sure you insert your earplugs and put your ear mufflers over them. You'll each have 100 rounds and we'll practice until 11:30, then we'll break for lunch and head back to headquarters for our afternoon meeting. If you run out of bullets just wave your paddle and I'll bring you more. I'll be your friendly range safety officer. Any questions?"

We were each assigned a Glock G42, a common law enforcement pistol. Our target was the typical drawing of a human torso and head, hanging from a frame. The picture was attached to an overhead wire so that it could be dragged to a shooter so he could see how his shots landed. Our directions were to aim for the torso.

"We'll start with a visual review with only one of you firing," said Buster. "The rest of you look at the target. Janice, how would you like to go first?" Buster would later tell us that he always went with the person he assumed was the least talented with a gun. That way he could use his criticism to instruct the others.

Janice opened fire. She squeezed off 12 rounds like she was shooting a squirt gun. Buster had the target pulled to us along the overhead line so we could get a better look. All 12 of her bullets hit within a tight circle no more than six inches in diameter. We all just stared.

"I think I'll go to the movies," said Buster. "If you guys have any questions just ask Madam James Bond over here."

We blasted away until 11:30 and then got into the bus for our trip back to the CIA headquarters building for lunch and our afternoon meeting.

Oliver Blake, Deputy to CIA Director Bill Carlini was waiting for us in the conference room.

"Agent Akhbar tells me that you all did well on the firing range this morning," said Blake, "especially Mrs. Monahan. I don't expect that you'll be unholstering your weapons at all, but you're not going to Disney World so we don't want to take any chances with your safety. This afternoon we're going to review the mission and your cover."

"Ollie," said Buster, "may I suggest a brief quiz on phone codes."

"Good idea, Buster. As you've been instructed you will text each other using codes, and you've also been told to memorize them. Dr. Weinberg, what's Mr. Burton's code?"

"That's Riordan, Seamus Riordan, my friend, and Wally's code is Bravo 929."

"Excellent," said Blake, "and thank you for correcting me about your newly adopted name."

Blake went back and forth quizzing us on our name codes and a few of our message codes, such as "Delta 911 – Need Assistance" or "Foxtrot 335 – I'm under fire," and especially "Zulu 566 – I have identified our suspect."

"First we'll review your cover," said Blake. "You're Canadian journalists working on a story about expatriated North Americans living in the Middle East. You'll each receive a briefing book about your fictional home city in case anybody asks you. The journalism angle should be easy for Mr. Burton and Mr. Thurber, who are both professional reporters. You'll be split into two groups, each led by one of our "real reporter." Mr. Thurber will team up with Mrs. Monahan and Mr. Burton will be with Dr. Wein... I mean Mr. Riordan."

Janice looked at me, smiled and winked.

"Each team will be tailed by two of our deep cover agents. If trouble starts, these guys know how to handle it. Here are their photos. Drill them into your heads so you don't think you're being tailed by a bad guy. Agent Akhbar – Buster, will be in overall charge of the mission."

"It can be hot as hell in Yemen, so we've picked out your clothing to account for that. You'll wear light khaki outfits. Ms. Monahan will wear a different outfit, one selected for extreme modesty. You don't need a full face covering, but your hair must be covered by a scarf at all times. Oh, and yes, Mrs. Monahan will be known as Mrs. Thurber, to avoid any problem with the religious cops fretting about a woman hanging around with a man who's not her husband."

"Great idea," said Janice as she slapped her hand on the table.

I just rubbed my face and thought about last night's Yankee game. At least she won't be dressed to accentuate her gorgeous body.

"Okay, so that's your cover," said Blake. "Now let's talk about the mission and its objective. It's really quite simple. We suspect that Joseph Monahan may be alive and living in Yemen. Our objective is to locate him, identify him, photograph him, and then call in your assigned agents to plant GPS devices. Your objective is not, I repeat

NOT, to engage him. You folks may have been deputized, but you're not trained CIA agents. Mrs. Monahan, especially, I'm sorry I mean Mrs. Thurber, should be very cautious if you've located the suspect. Obviously, you don't want him to notice you. We want to gather information on this guy, evidence if you will, and eventually give it all to Mr. Thurber, for reasons that haven't been explained to me. We've got to consider Monahan dangerous. If he's who we think he is, he's a man who wants to kill an aircraft carrier full of people in cold blood. Again, our objective is not to bring him to justice. That will come later, and I don't doubt that a Seal Team is already getting set for that mission. Any questions?"

"As a reporter," I said, "I already have a few ideas, but have you folks thought about where we should start?"

"Great question," said Blake. "You'll be staying at the Hotel Al Saeed in downtown Sanaa. It's about as upscale a place you'll find in the country. Running water, flush toilets, top shelf booze, the whole bit. It's crawling with western types, business people, lawyers, and probably a few journalists. Your job will be to chat, tell them about your newspaper assignment, and let the conversation take you places."

"Does the hotel have a gym?" I asked.

"Yes, a good one, with all the equipment you can think of."

"Great," said Janice.

"But it's strictly segregated. Men behind one wall, women behind the other. The Hotel Al Saeed may be sort of Western but only *sort of.*"

"You will report to Langley once a day at 8 PM local time. That job will be for Mr. Riordan over here. Ben has worked with us many times and he knows the drill. He'll report via encrypted email from a computer we'll place in his room. I recommend that he confer with all of you before sending his nightly message. Okay with you Mr. Riordan?" Bennie nodded.

"Ollie," said Buster, "may I suggest you call these folks by their first names?"

"Good idea, Buster. Sometimes I sound a little too Fed. Okay, Jack, Wally, Janice, and Ben...I mean Seamus, it's time to pick up your briefing books and do some studying back at your hotel. Tomorrow after the gun range you'll be taken to the medical department for your inoculations. After that we'll have another meeting here. Today's Wednesday. You leave on Friday. You'll know your flight times by tomorrow's meeting. Study hard my friends."

CHAPTER 23

We all agreed to meet for supper at 6:30 after we hit the gym at the Marriott. Wally and Ben (Seamus) aren't fitness nuts like Janice and me, but they agreed to join me because they know our trip is going to be physically demanding. Bennie's really out of shape so I coached him to take it slow in the beginning. He and Wally will be able to continue their newfound fitness routine when we get to the Hotel Al Saeed in Yemen.

We got a table at the back of the dining room so we could talk in privacy.

"I can't believe I'm 45 years old," said Bennie, "spent the morning at a firing range, then went to a gym, and I'm about to play Agent 007 in some fleabag country. And we're going through all this shit so our friend Jack can leave us and head back to the past to save the world. Maybe I'm crazy, but I'm kind of enjoying this."

"Since my worthless turd of a husband disappeared," said Janice, "my life had become a bore. I have enough engineering projects to keep me busy but it's become a grinding routine. I agree with Ben, this is actually fun. It will really be fun if we find my mass-murdering hubby."

"I have to agree," said Wally. "I love my job at the *Times* and I get to write about fascinating stuff, but this is like nothing I ever imagined. A reporter lives on curiosity, and my God we've got a lot to be curious about. I've been all over the world on assignments, like Jack, but now I feel like I've been written into a movie script. How do you feel, Jack?"

"Well," I said, "I agree with all of you about the excitement of it all. But I have something in the pit of my stomach that I don't think you guys have. You're all thinking, 'we can do this,' but I'm thinking, we've GOT to do this. Remember, I come at this whole thing from the weird prospective of a time traveler. I saw the last moment of my life on that video, and my wife's last moment as well, not to mention a few thousand others. I need to change that. With the help of you guys I *will* change it. What the world will look like when I'm successful, I have no idea. But it can't be as fucked up as it is now, can it?"

CHAPTER 24

My name is Lieutenant Commander Ralph Martin, weapons officer of the *USS Carl Vinson*. But don't call me Ralph or Mr. Martin. Call me Fatah Zayyaf, my true name, my Muslim name, a name that gives praise to Allah.

I guess I don't sound like a typical American naval officer. I'm supposed to be a proud American patriot. I'm supposed to be a Roman Catholic. I'm supposed to be a simple American family man. I'm supposed to be a lot of things that I'm not. My wife Barbara knows nothing about me although we've been married for 10 years. She thinks that I'm the man I pretend to be, and that's exactly how I've played it all these years. In high school and college I was a good student and active in sports, especially baseball. I was the pitcher for my school team in my senior year. Of course I dated girls and used them for my pleasure, which is the way of the infidel.

Ever since my high school trip to Riyadh, my life has not just changed, it's taken on a meaning that my infidel acquaintances will never know. The trip was sponsored by *The Center for Open-Minded Youth* and funded by the government of Saudi Arabia. In Riyadh, I met a man who not only changed my life, but a man who showed me the true meaning of life. Sheik Ayham Abboud is my spiritual light. He was my mentor as well as the guide to my four friends who made the trip with me. Sheik Abboud taught us that the journey of life need not be dependent on circumstances. He showed us that a true spiritual path ignores the day-to-day-crap that life throws at us. He also taught us that jihad in the name of Allah is the highest calling a man can hear.

My four American brothers also heard the call and we all converted to Islam by the time our visit was over. The path of truth and righteousness was ours.

In a few weeks my brothers and I will unleash hell on American targets. Some of the infidels will call it terrorism, some even murder. But what they don't know is that our actions will be cleansed by Allah, sanctified in his name, and justified by his truth.

CHAPTER 25

On Friday the four of us arrived at Kennedy Airport. Wally and Ben were scheduled to fly to Riyadh, Saudi Arabia at 11 AM and make a connecting flight to Sanaa, Yemen. Janice and I were scheduled to fly to Doha, Qatar at 1 PM and to connect to Sanaa an hour after we landed. None of us knew how and where Buster was going – he has a flair for secrecy – but we were supposed to rendezvous with him at the Hotel Al Saeed in Yemen on Saturday. We were all booked on Delta Airlines flights, so we could ease into our third world journey in American comfort.

While we awaited our flights, Ben, Wally, and myself took the opportunity to comment on Janice's new makeover, courtesy of the CIA Clandestine Ops Unit.

"How'd we wind up with such a homely teammate?" said Wally.

"Are you the Janice Monahan who used to be good looking?" chimed in Bennie.

"Hey, blond hair and makeup are overrated," I said. "Nothing like a full body gown to stir the senses."

"Okay, wise-asses," said Janice. "You're looking at the me that my wonderful hubby wanted."

* * *

"I'm not believing this," said Janice as the plane lifted off the runway. "Two weeks ago I was a simple engineer working on an HVAC system for a bank in New Jersey. Now here I am on a hunt for international terrorists."

I put my finger to my lips to let her know not to talk so loud. She nodded.

"You're a brave, patriotic woman, Janice. You didn't have to get yourself involved in all of this."

She looked into my eyes and stroked my arm. Shit – I didn't mean that as a come-on, just a simple compliment. I closed my eyes and thought about Ashley. I'm a monogamous guy, simple as that. Simple, but not always easy.

"How could I not get involved in this, Jack? As Joe and I grew more distant, as his religious zeal started to color everything in our lives, my love for the guy turned to tolerance. Then my tolerance turned to contempt, and after what you guys have told me, I'm starting to feel serious hatred. It bothers me to say that, but the man betrayed me and the entire country. I felt like a mantel ornament in his life. I want to find him as much as you do Jack, maybe more."

Our need to speak softly forced us to move our heads close to each other because of the flight noise. After a slight turbulence, our foreheads touched. Where did she get that perfume?

Okay, *the Yankees are up in the bottom of the seventh. Breslow's pitching for the Red Sox and the Yankees have Ellsbury at the plate. The count is two and two.* I looked at my watch. Thirteen hours to go.

I dozed off and was in a deep sleep when I felt a hand gently stroking my face.

"Jack, I forgot to tell you something."

Great, now I suppose she wants to get a room as soon as we land.

"Today's my birthday. Thirty-seven, young enough to still admit it. How old are you, Jack?"

"I'm 37 too, as of four months ago. Happy birthday, Janice. We'll all have to celebrate when we get to the hotel in Yemen."

"I thought just you and I might have a quiet drink together."

"Janice, remember, we're a team. Counting Wally, Ben, and Buster that's five. We work, think, and talk together. Yeah, and we drink together too."

"Sorry I woke you," Janice said. "I'm just having a hard time sleeping or reading. My mind just keeps racing."

"I understand," I said. "I'm a bit on edge myself. But we should try to snooze. We have a lot to do when we arrive."

I dozed off again for a half hour or so. Somebody was stroking my hand.

"Thought of something else, Janice?"

"I don't want to make you feel sad or anything, but, well, tell me about Ashley."

"You won't make me feel sad at all. Worried, maybe, but not sad. Remember, Ashley is very much alive, and I intend to keep it that way. So what can I tell you about Ashley that you haven't already read in the newspapers and magazines? We met in the weirdest of circumstances. She was the Captain of the guided missile cruiser *USS California* and I was a junior officer on the ship. Actually she promoted me to commissioned officer. I was an enlisted man."

"You were an enlisted man, with all your academic degrees and experience?"

"Long story. As you know, the ship slipped through a time portal or wormhole and wound up at the start of the Civil War. You know the rest. One of the biggest stories ever."

"But tell me about Ashley."

"Well, it's a love story. We met constantly because I was the author of that book *Living History – Stories of Time Travel Through the Ages*. I was the only one on the ship who knew anything about time travel. After a while Ashley and I would meet just to be with each other. We were about the same age and something just clicked. By the time four months had gone by, four months of 1861 time that is, we had fallen in love. Ashley is an amazing woman. She's a tough military leader, a visionary thinker, and the sweetest, most feminine woman I've ever known. So I ended my brief Navy career and we got married. I went back to journalism and she took command of a nuclear aircraft carrier, the next logical step before she becomes an admiral. I've only been gone a short time, but I miss her a lot. We're not just married lovers, we're good friends. Does that sound corny?"

"No, it doesn't Jack. You two had a wonderful thing. I'm jealous of the both of you."

"Janice, Ashley and I *have* a wonderful thing, present tense. It's not over, not if I have anything to do with it. And don't be jealous of our happiness. We can't figure out fate any easier than we can figure out time. If I were writing a story, a remarkable woman like you would have married a wonderful guy and had a great life. You can still have a great life."

"Maybe, as long as I'm not involved with that prick. Let me ask you something, Jack. Didn't you say that you were writing a book about the *Gray Ship* incident?"

"Yes, it was about half way done when I slipped through the wormhole."

"When it's published, I want a signed copy."

"Absolutely. I'll write, 'To Janice, my good friend and teammate.'"

"I'd like that, Jack, I really would."

I thought she was going to kiss me. Instead, she gave me a gentle punch to my arm. She sat back and I noticed a tear run down her face. Janice is a good woman, and she deserves better than the creep she married. I can't imagine how she lives with such a crushing disloyalty. Joe Monahan not only betrayed Janice, he betrayed his country. He was willing to commit murder, mass murder, for a twisted idea. If there is such a thing as evil, he personifies it. Janice is a survivor, a smart, gutsy survivor with a lot of character.

I'm glad we had this talk, and I'm glad she brought the subject up. Janice and I could easily have a serious relationship. I think I convinced her that Ashley is the woman of my life.

CHAPTER 26

Janice and I landed in Doha, Qatar at noon local time. From the airport we could see the beautiful architecture of the city, not to mention the airport itself. Although not as skyscraper crazy as Dubai, UAE, Doha is a striking city.

"Don't get too used to the glistening buildings Janice," I said. "Sanaa isn't like this. It's one of the oldest cities in the world, and Yemen isn't modern like Qatar. Too bad your husband didn't take a liking to this place."

"Making bad decisions is in his blood," Janice said.

We made our connecting flight to Sanaa, Yemen an hour later and landed at 2:20 PM. Buster had arranged for a car to pick us up, and we checked into the Hotel Al Saeed at 4 PM. My body screamed for exercise so I headed for the gym right after I checked into my room. Janice did the same, in the women's gym of course. Because Janice and I were supposedly married, our one room was in my name. I bunked with Bennie.

We arranged to meet Wally and Ben in the dining room at 6:30. Buster, our clandestine CIA team leader didn't want to be seen with us. Our waiter, a classy guy who could easily fit in at the Four Seasons, handed us our menus and called our attention to the specials on photocopied sheets. The "specials" were instructions from Buster. The waiter gave us a wink, and took our drink orders. I've had a lot of doubts about the efficiency of the CIA, but they were starting to evaporate. We ordered our drinks, a beer for me, wine for Janice, Irish whiskey on the rocks for Bennie, and a martini for Wally.

"I didn't think Jews like to drink hard liquor, Bennie," whispered Wally with a laugh.

"The name's Seamus, shithead," said Ben.

"Sorry Seamus Shithead," said Wally.

The four of us laughed hysterically, much more than we should have from a simple joke. The stress of travel and our thoughts about the mission ahead took their toll. We laughed until we cried.

While we nursed our drinks, hors d'oeuvres were served, four different variations of lamb, cooked to perfection. Buster knows how to pick hotels.

As we finished the hors d'oeuvres, a loud noise shattered the pleasant atmosphere. A dozen glasses and assorted dinnerware flew across the room directly in front of us, launched from an overturned table. A guy with his head and face covered by a scarf stood at the entrance, holding an AK 47 and screaming in Arabic. He cocked his gun, chambering the first round. I'm a writer, not a warrior. I froze, as did everybody else in the dining room.

Well, not everyone. Janice, almost casually, slipped off her seat in one fluid motion and dropped to the floor on her right knee. She aimed her Glock with both hands and fired three shots, one to the man's head and two to his torso. The dining room fell silent.

The hotel manager came running into the room. He screamed in broken English, "Everything okay my friends. Ees a crazy man. We fire him from keetchen yesterday and he come here for to make revenge. Pleez relax. Drinks on house."

As he spoke the gunman's body was dragged from the room and kitchen staff busied themselves cleaning up the glass and blood. I found it strangely comforting to see that the manager's first response to the mayhem was to ensure good customer service.

Sharif, our waiter/CIA operative came to our table and said, "Welcome to Yemen. Happens all the time. Great aim. Who shot that guy?"

Bennie raised his hand immediately and said, "It was me." Bennie had quickly surmised that a gun slinging woman was not a favored character in Yemen.

"Everything's okay, folks," said Sharif. "Now please, let me take your main course orders."

"I'll have what she's having," Wally said.

We all laughed, if you can believe it.

We picked at our main course. Having almost gotten killed and watching our lovely teammate calmly blow away the bad guy did nothing for our appetites. Exhausted from travel and the stress of the evening's gunfire, we headed for our rooms, making sure to keep our firearms handy on our night tables.

CHAPTER 27

The next morning at 9 AM, a driver picked us up in a white Toyota SUV, the vehicle of choice throughout the Middle East because the Japanese are efficient at supplying spare parts. Our destination was a safe house about a half hour from the hotel, where we would meet with Team Leader Buster. It was a modest-sized nondescript house of cement block with a small garden in front. The driver pulled the SUV to the back of the house where we entered after he made sure we weren't seen.

"So I understand you got an official Yemeni welcome at dinner last night," said Buster with a broad grin. "Nice shot Bennie, I mean Seamus."

"It was me," said Janice.

"I figured it would be bad form to have people think a woman did the deed," said Bennie.

"Good move, Seamus," said Buster. "You people are a lot better than I expected. Janice, if you ever get tired of designing air conditioners, I can promise you a bright career at the CIA."

"Buster," I said, "I can't believe there was no police investigation of the incident. None of us were interrogated by anyone."

"Welcome to Yemen, my friends. Sharif told me what happened after the shooting. It was a typical Yemeni police procedure. A cop shows up and interviews the hotel manager. The manager tells him the gunman was a disgruntled employee and was looking for some pay back. He then tells the cop that the gunman was shot by an Irish-Canadian guy, as he slips him a hundred bucks. Case closed. Another chapter in the annals of Yemeni justice."

"To change the conversation to a more peaceful subject, I think we have an important lead, or at least a source," said Buster. "One of our operatives met an Australian guy named Trevor McMartin. He's a bank examiner and has been on assignment in Yemen for over three years. He tracks down dirty money, the people who handle it, and where the money goes. His parents are from the Middle East and he looks Arabic, and speaks it fluently. Trevor McMartin goes by the name Salem Yousef. We've checked him out with our sources in Australia and he's the real deal, solid as rock and a sharp investigator. He mainly looks for western money that finds its way here. He's very good at his job, knows where to look and where not to look, and gets paid a load of dough. Our operative told him that he knows some Canadian journalists doing a story on western expats to Yemen, and maybe McMartin would like to meet them. We've arranged for all four of you to meet him at the Holiday Inn Mukalla here in Sanaa. Seamus, I want you to strap on your bullshit detector hat. This guy may be very helpful. Okay, you're scheduled to meet him in an hour. We'll get together again here tomorrow. Try not to shoot anybody, Janice."

"Not unless absolutely necessary," said Janice.

I think she's really getting to like this spy stuff.

CHAPTER 28

Janice Monahan here. I never shot anybody before, never even aimed at someone. I'm a good shot with a pistol, even better with a rifle. My dad, a retired Marine sergeant, would take me to the shooting range a lot. He believed that everybody, especially women, should know how to handle a gun. Our evening in the restaurant at the Hotel Al Saeed convinced me that Dad was right.

Killing is a strange feeling, it leaves a lingering creepiness, and comes back shattering into your consciousness when you least expect it. I now understand how soldiers can suffer from PTSD. There's nothing nice about shooting someone, but if I didn't have my Glock on me, we all may have been killed. If we were in some politically correct "gun free zone" in the States we'd just be entries in a police blotter. I think there's something to the idea that if guns were made illegal, only criminals would have them. I don't think that nut at the Al Saeed would have been persuaded by a local ordinance and a gun-free sign. I'm not happy about killing the guy, but I don't feel guilty. I'm alive, and so are my friends.

So here we are with Jack on our quest to find information on the Atomic Five, one of whom is my murderous bastard of a husband. The sooner we can gather the evidence Jack needs, the sooner we can go back to the States, and the sooner Jack can find the wormhole.

Jack has finally convinced me of this weird thing called time travel. I've bought into this business of Jack going back to 2015 to prevent the Thanksgiving Attacks. I accept the idea that time is a dimension through which a human being can slip. I love the idea that a national tragedy can be prevented, and that 26,000 lives, including Jack's and Ashley's, can be saved.

But I'm having a bitch of a time coming to grips with something that goes along with all of that good stuff. I'm having a hard time buying the idea that Jack Thurber will soon disappear from my life, a really hard time. Okay, I've accepted the idea that Jack can save Ashley's life and his own, and that they can live happily ever after. I know this sounds selfish—the petulant musings of a brat who wants things her way – but I feel like crap.

I know exactly what I'm *supposed* to feel. I'm supposed to be happy that Jack Thurber will return to the past and save the day. Obviously that's how I should feel. But the shitty thing about feelings is that you don't have control over them, they show up as if you wanted them to be there. My dominant feeling is the pain over the sad fact that I'll lose Jack, and I'm ashamed of that feeling. But how can I be ashamed of a feeling that's just there, a feeling that I'm not conjuring up. I didn't put it there, it's just there.

I hate it when people make victims of themselves, and I feel like I'm doing just that. The fact that my murderous scumbag of a husband betrayed me and his country infuriates me. This is where I start to feel like a victim, but I'm not. I've got to look at it as a circumstance in my life, one that I had nothing to do with, but one that shouldn't make me a whimpering fool.

I think it's time to get a grip and be an adult.

All of this is exciting.

It also sucks.

CHAPTER 29

The Holiday Inn Mukalla wasn't as upscale as the Al Saeed Hotel, but it was typical of Holiday Inn standards, never opulent but always clean and efficient. We walked into the lobby and I told the clerk we were there to meet a Mr. Salem Yousef. The clerk gestured us toward a meeting room down a corridor. Strong coffee and light snacks awaited us, along with Trevor McMartin.

Bennie strolled around the room, feigning back pain and checking his email. What he was checking was a device that detects electronic bugs.

The man was impeccably dressed in a tan summer suit. He wore a blue shirt and an orange tie. He even sported a fresh cut flower in his lapel. His shoes alone must have cost over a thousand bucks.

I introduced the four of us and I asked if we could call him Trevor.

"G'day, mates, and yes please call me Trevor (*Trevah*)." The guy looked like Omar Shariff but sounded like Crocodile Dundee. "Yes, my local name is Salem Yousef, but I prefer my Anglican name Trevor McMartin, not that I get to use it around here very often."

We exchanged pleasantries, discussing the weather and the highlights of Yemen. We had agreed not to jump right into discussing our reason for being there, because that would immediately tag us as Americans, not Canadians. Americans have a way of delivering an elevator speech and getting down to business quickly. But we're Canadians, or at least that's our cover. Trevor had an expansive, friendly personality, but I noticed that whenever he wasn't sure what you were asking, his eyes would narrow and focus like lasers.

"I think you've been told, Trevor," I said, "that we're doing a feature length article for the *Toronto Star* about Canadians and Americans who have relocated to Yemen, other than for government or business reasons."

"You mean your readers are curious why a bloke would leave the beauty of Canada or the States and take up residence in this cesspool?"

"You get the idea, Trevor," I said. "People expatriate themselves all the time, but usually for a nicer location like Fiji, Switzerland, or Australia for that matter. We're trying to get a handle on why people come here. We've heard of retired businessmen, politicians and even military personnel coming here. We're trying to track some of these people down and interview them. We're especially interested in military types. Why would a former soldier or sailor move to a country that's in a state of undeclared war with his country. Do you find that strange?"

"Yes, I do, mate. I have a hard time believing that a Canadian or an American, or any western military person, would come here for any reason. My job is to track down money, but you can't separate the money from other motives. I mean why would a soldier give up his Western freedoms and come to this rat hole?"

"Have you heard of any specific military people who have immigrated here?" Wally asked, trying affect an off-hand manner.

"Yeah, one guy sticks out in my mind," said Trevor. The fella calls himself Abu Hussein, I believe. I can check that for you. He's a former American naval officer, I've discovered, who showed up here about two years ago. I know about him because he's got a huge fucking bankroll, which is what caught my attention."

"Do you recall his American name, Trevor?" asked Janice.

"Give me a minute, Luv. First name starts with a "J," James, John, Joseph — yes, Joseph it is. Last name is Morgan, McLaughlin, Mangan or something. Wait, no, it's Monahan, yes, Joseph Monahan, aka Abu Hussein."

Each of us struggled to keep our jaws from dropping and we all started to perspire. Janice kept twisting a napkin as if she was trying to kill it.

"Hey, mates, ya want me to turn down the a/c a bit?"

"That would be great, Trevor," I said.

"Have you personally seen him?" Janice asked, trying to sound casual.

"Of course. I'm a very hands-on money tracker. I once tailed this bloke for a week, going in and out of big American and Swiss banks. He handles a lot of money. What the hell he's doing here is beyond my imagination. I've stood near him when he was speaking to someone. His Arabic is lousy, but he tries hard."

"You say he handles a lot of money, Trevor. Any idea where it comes from?" asked Ben/Seamus.

"No I don't, but it definitely comes from and goes to the Middle East. He's a classic money launderer. One day his account is in the millions, the next it's down to a few thousand, American dollars that is. I have no idea what he's doing with the money, but he's funneling it to somebody or something."

"Any chance that you have a photo of him, Trevor?" asked Janice, still trying to strangle her napkin.

"Sure, I have a bunch right here. I'm stupid to carry these around with me, but I had an idea what you folks were looking for."

Trevor took out an envelope from his briefcase with about a dozen photos of Monahan. He handed them to me and I passed them around. When they got to Janice, she got off her chair suddenly, said that she had too much coffee that morning, and would be right back. We could hear her vomiting through the closed bathroom door. The remaining three of us simultaneously cleared our throats to muffle the sound. Trevor's eyes narrowed.

Janice returned, her face whiter than the tablecloth. She apologized and sat down.

The photos came back to me and I leafed through them. One showed Monahan in front of the Yemen Gulf Bank, another in front of the National Bank of Yemen. I held in my hands the most dramatic evidence of Monahan and his whereabouts I could possibly imagine.

"Can we have copies of these?" I asked Trevor.

"No worry, mate, just don't tell anybody where you got them."

"Are they time and date stamped?" I asked.

"They're all digital on my hard drive. Just click preferences and you get a time and date stamp."

My heart was pounding. This was too good to be true. When Buster said he had a good source he had no idea just how good he was. We didn't even need to meet Monahan. Trevor had taken care of that.

"Trevor, we have a few other names that have been floating around," I said. "Mind if I pass them by you?" Trevor agreed.

"George Quentin, aka Jazeer Mohammed?"

"He showed up on my radar about a year ago. Last I knew he was in Riyadh, Saudi Arabia. Another big bank account that grew and shrank daily. Here's a few pictures." One of the photos showed Quentin entering the Riyadh Bank.

"Ralph Martin, aka Fatah Zayyaf?"

"He was here in Sanaa about six months ago. I think, yes here it is, a picture of him and Monahan in front of the Yemen Gulf Bank."

"Frederick Peyton, aka Lashkar Islamiyah?"

"Him, I don't know. Let me jot down his names. Maybe you folks are doing me a favor too."

"Philip Murphy, aka Mohammed Hussein?"

"Last I saw of him was in Cairo, Egypt. Here's a picture of him with a big man from the Muslim Brotherhood."

Hoping I wasn't being too pushy, I asked Trevor if he could email all the photos so I could have digital copies on my laptop. He said he wouldn't trust email, but that he would back up all the photos onto a flash drive and give them to me the next morning.

"Trevor, my friend, we can't thank you enough. Now we just have to locate these men to interview them," I lied. I knew we couldn't interview them, but the photos were enough, if not for a newspaper article.

"Do yourselves a favor, mates. If you really want to interview these blokes, come up with a better line of bullshit than the Canadian newspaper article nonsense. You folks aren't Canadian newspaper reporters any more than I'm Queen Elizabeth. You're Americans, and you're CIA, and that's fine by me. I love your country and I hate traitors and I'm glad to help out. Just remember, you can't bullshit me and you can't bullshit them. You're about to stick your dicks into a snake pit – whoops, my apologies, Janice. Be careful, my friends. Call me if you need any more help."

We said goodbye to our Aussie friend, our new best friend.

CHAPTER 30

Our car pulled to the back of the safe house, where Buster was waiting for us. Once inside, Buster motioned us to a table covered with water, soft drinks, and light snacks.

"How did your meeting with Trevor go?" Buster asked.

"That one meeting made this entire trip worth it," I said. "Thanks to Trevor, we should be ready to wrap up the mission tomorrow and head back to New York." We told Buster about the photos, the identifications, and the time verified locations of all but one of the targets. I told him that Trevor had already done what we had set out to do.

"Do you have the photos?" asked Buster.

"Yes, here they are. But they're not time and date stamped. That's why I'm seeing Trevor tomorrow so he can give me a flash drive with copies of all the photos including time and date stamps. I'm meeting him at 9 AM at his hotel."

"I don't like it," said Buster. "Trevor has been around here for years and knows the ropes as well as a spook, but chances are he's been seen with you guys. I'll send one of our operatives to pick up the flash drive. Call Trevor and tell him. Here's the name and description of our guy. You stay put, Jack."

CHAPTER 31

My name is Frederick Peyton. I'm a 39-year-old naval officer and the weapons officer of the *USS Theodore Roosevelt*. It's no coincidence that I'm in charge of the ship's weapons department, an assignment I have been planning for almost twenty years. In the military, things get done by taking orders. But knowing one's way around can get you position you want, maybe not the exact ship, but the right department.

It isn't like I'm overly fond of weapons, but my position on the ship is critical to my mission. Yes, I have a mission, and not one that the Navy shares. It isn't a mission the Navy assigned to me, or one that a superior officer dreamed up. I am on a mission of Allah. My rank says lieutenant commander, but my most proud title is simply jihadi.

It wasn't a straight path without detours. Five years after my awakening on a high school trip to Riyadh, I returned to the darkness of the heathen infidels. I became an alcoholic and a drug abuser at the age of 23. I was a naval officer at the time and managed to hide my afflictions from my superiors, but I could not hide them from myself. My marriage was ruined and my life became a pursuit of elusive pleasure. I had turned my back on Allah and I was paying for it. One day the beloved Sheik Abboud called me. He was my spiritual guide and mentor on my trip to Riyadh, a man who had the most profound influence on my life. We met in a park near the pier where my ship was berthed. Just as he did in Riyadh, Sheik Abboud reached in and spoke to my soul. He reminded me of my glorious conversion to Islam when I was a youth of 18, and how Islam changed my world and put me on the path of truth. He also reminded me of the sacred pact that my four young friends and I made those long years ago, a pact to become jihadis in the war against the infidel. He also reminded me of my long-term goal, to be one of the shells in the canon that would blast the heathen hearts of the enemies of Islam. He reminded me why I was in the Navy, and reminded me that I had been specially chosen for our holy mission.

With the guidance of Sheik Abboud I tossed aside the habits of the infidel and redirected my soul toward heaven. He relit the fire that burned in me on that trip to Riyadh, a fire that burns brighter every day. Soon the apostates will feel the heat of my sacred fire.

I resumed my double life thanks to Sheik Abboud, the life that was one part all-American naval officer and the other part a warrior in the cause of Islam. The blessed trust that has been placed in me will help bring a new life to the world, a new caliphate, a world ruled by the law of Allah.

And I have been chosen to be a key in the plan to bring about the new just world.

CHAPTER 32

The Thanksgiving Gang had breakfast at the Al Saeed Hotel at 7:30 AM the next day. It was one of our happiest meals together. Within days we would all head back to New York, and I would catch the wormhole express back to 2015 with my evidence. A waiter came to our table and said that a man was holding for me on the lobby phone. I picked up the phone. It was Buster.

"The four of you come to the safe house immediately – NOW," said Buster.

Our car pulled up to the back of the house. Buster was pacing in the living room when we entered. I'd never seen Buster visibly upset before. He looked like somebody who had to pee but couldn't find a bathroom. Buster motioned for us to sit.

"I just met with our operative," said Buster, "the guy who was supposed to get the flash drive from Trevor. Well, Trevor's missing. Nobody at the hotel knows where he is. His room's been ransacked and his computer's gone. We have to assume the worst, an assumption I don't want to make, but one that's obvious. Trevor's been kidnapped and probably murdered."

None of us spoke. Besides the great information he gave us, we had all taken a personal liking to Trevor. It was like hearing that your good friend had been kidnapped. Well, that's exactly what happened.

"So we're back to square one," I said. "We have to find the bombers and take our own pictures."

"Absolutely not, no fucking way," said Buster. "It's probably obvious to you that the Agency had a plan B. If your magical trip backwards doesn't work, we'll have to track these guys down and take them out to prevent a future attack. But If your plan to return to 2015 does work, then it's a moot question. In our time, there will never have been the Thanksgiving Attack. We just don't have enough time to find these guys and get you back to 2015. The photos you have will do, they'll have to. Hell, you're not going on trial, you just have to convince some people, especially your wife, Captain Patterson, that you know what will happen on Thanksgiving Day. You guys are going back to New York ASAP. We're gonna fly you on a CIA jet to Kuwait City, where you'll catch a U.S. military plane back to the States. The fact that Trevor got kidnapped tells us that the cover is blown, and I have to assume that you people are now targets. You'll be picked up at the Al Saeed Hotel at 1 PM, two hours from now and I'll be with you. Headquarters at Langley thinks I may be in the crosshairs too. We'll travel to the airport in two cars. Make sure to have your weapons handy. Okay, let's get moving."

CHAPTER 33

At the Airport in Kuwait City we boarded a Lockheed C-141 Starlifter, the biggest plane any of us had ever seen. Buster has a professional habit of giving us only the information we need to know, so he couldn't answer our questions about why we should be on such a large plane. He just told us that the plane was delivering goods marked "none of your business" back to the States. An hour after take-off, we huddled in the huge passenger space for a meeting. Buster had seen to it that we had a well-stocked bar at our disposal. Buster is a full-service spook. We sat around a make-shift conference table, nursing our drinks. The flight was amazingly smooth, the gigantic plane casually flicking off cross winds.

"Jack, you've convinced the Directors of the FBI and CIA, not to mention myself, about this time travel stuff. I'm authorized to tell you that the Agency is at your side and we'll do anything we can to help. But I need to know something. How does it work?"

"Well," I said, "I can only go from past experience with this weird phenomenon. Time portals or wormholes are physical locations throughout the earth. Some people, like me, have a strange habit of stepping on them. When the *USS California* tripped into the past during that *Gray Ship* incident, it was something new for me. We had to find a spot in the ocean, not an easy job. When I stepped on that grate on the East Side of Manhattan, it was a more traditional, if that's a good way of putting it, wormhole. What I have to do now is reverse the procedure. I have plenty of photos of the spot to help me to locate it. I just have to go back to the grate and step on it, and if my past experiences mean anything, I'll find myself back in July 2015, about 4 months before the Thanksgiving Attacks."

"You've been here in 2017 for just shy of a month, Jack," said Bennie. "I guess there's been a full tilt search going on for you."

"That's another weird thing about this business," I said. "In my book, as you well know Bennie, all of the people who time travelled found that the time in the past was very short compared to the place they came from. Remember that one guy who went from 1987 to the First World War and spent seven months on the fields of France. When he came back he had only been gone for five minutes. The same thing happened to the *California*. We spent four months in the year 1861 and when we came back to 2013 only seven hours had gone by."

"Yeah, but this time you travelled to the future," said Wally. "Do you think that will make a difference?"

"I have no idea," I said. "I don't know if time travels slower in *my* 2015 or maybe even faster. If it's faster, I'm worried. When I hit the wormhole it was about four months before the attacks. If time moves slow then I'll have plenty of time to get the job done. If it goes faster, the job will be a lot more exciting."

"I could use another vodka," said Janice.

"So what's the plan, Jack?" said Buster. "I'm sure you're not going to walk around with a sign saying, 'repent, the time is near.'"

"Ashley Patterson is the simple answer," I said. "Ashley's a very influential woman. She's the youngest person to command a nuclear aircraft carrier, not to mention the first woman and the first black woman to hold that position. She's going to make admiral soon. People listen to her, including people at the White House. And I don't have to convince Ashley about the reality of time travel. Remember, we met in 1861."

As I said that, my friends shook their heads like dogs climbing out of water. They all knew it. They all bought it. But they all had a hard time believing it. I don't blame them. I have a hard time believing it myself.

CHAPTER 34

Our plane landed at JFK at 7 AM. We decided to meet in Wally's office at the *Times* that afternoon at 1 PM, giving us enough time to freshen up after our flight.

I was 20 minutes late after my workout at the gym. When I got to Wally's office a light lunch of assorted wraps and salads had just been served.

"Jack," said Wally, "I have a big question. Assuming that you're successful in pulling this off and preventing the attacks, what happens to our reality here in 2017? Take a look at this."

Wally circulated copies of an article he had written six months ago about the press coverage given to the Thanksgiving Attacks.

"There have been more articles and TV spots devoted to the attacks than any event in human history," Wally said, "more than 9/11, the Iraq war, or Afghanistan. The Thanksgiving Attacks have become part of our history, but even more than that, they've become part of our consciousness. Every time we're stopped by a cop to see our 'papers' we remember Thanksgiving Day 2015. So what I'm asking is, do we just suddenly forget? Will the attacks just be erased from our collective memories?"

"Look," I said, "all I can tell you is what I experienced. In the *Gray Ship* incident, an entire crew of the *USS California* was away from the year 2013 for seven hours in 2013 time and spent four months in 1861. We changed the course of the Civil War. When we came back to 2013 it was a different 2013. History had changed and people's recollections had changed with it. So, yeah, if I pull this off, none of you will remember the Thanksgiving Attacks, because they will never have happened."

* * *

"Jack, the three of us have been conspiring," said Bennie with a nervous smile. "We started talking about this on the plane when you were sleeping, and we continued the conversation before you got here."

"So what's the big conspiracy, Bennie?" I asked.

"We all want to go back with you, back to 2015," said Ben. "None of us are married, except for Janice and I don't think she much gives a shit about her husband. We have no kids, we're flexible. You're planning to go back with a bunch of non-dated photos. We want to be part of your evidence, a big part."

"You can't pull this off alone, Jack," said Wally.

"It's no time to break up the team," said Janice.

So we agreed. We'd all make the trip to 2015, or at least try.

"Okay," I said. "I have my doubts about this, but you all make a good point. The critical thing is to accomplish the mission, to stop the attacks. Let's meet at the vacant lot over on the East Side tomorrow. Then let's plan to cross the wormhole the following morning."

CHAPTER 35

The next morning we met at Bennie's office and took Wally's car to the vacant lot on 119th Street. Construction trucks were parked bumper to bumper along the curb, making it hard to see the field until we got to a curb cut.

Suddenly, the bottom dropped out of my life. The empty lot that was here three weeks ago was now a beehive of construction activity. A dozen bulldozers worked the soil at the far end of the site. Three large cranes were dropping dirt into dump trucks. I tried to get my bearings as best as I could, but the look of the site had changed since I last saw it. I took some photos of the wormhole out of my pocket and tried to line it up with what was going on in front of me. From one of the pictures, a Bank of America sign was clearly visible in the near distance. I lined myself up with the sign, and the blood started to return to my brain. There was the wormhole, not yet disturbed by the earth moving equipment.

A construction foreman approached us, yelling over the din of the machines.

"You people are going to have to clear out of here," he said. "We'll be working on this section next."

"You can't dig here yet," I said. I was blunt but entirely unpersuasive.

"Why not?" he shouted.

"It's hard to explain," I explained. "It's a matter of national security."

"If you people don't leave here immediately I'm calling the cops. I don't have to tell you what that will mean."

"Okay, let's move outside the curb," I said to the team. The last thing we needed was a time wasting confrontation, and possibly jail if the police showed up.

"We need clout, Jack, some big clout," said Bennie. "Let's get the FBI Director on the phone."

We got inside Wally's car and I dialed the number of FBI Director Watson. The person who answered the phone told me that the Director could not be disturbed because she was in a high level meeting.

"Please tell her it's Jack Thurber — she knows me — and tell her it's absolutely urgent."

"I'm sorry Mr. Thurber but I have strict orders not to disturb the Director. If you give me your number I'll make sure she calls you back."

Shouting seldom works, especially with government types. I took a deep breath and said, "Please tell Director Watson that it's a matter of life and death and an immediate threat to national security. I repeat that the threat is *immediate*."

"Okay, said the assistant, I'll put you through. My job is on the line."

That's an amazing thing to ponder. A federal employee actually getting fired.

Sarah Watson abruptly left the meeting and went into the hallway to take my call. I told her what was happening and that we needed to somehow get a stop work order.

Watson placed a call to the Mayor of New York City, who was also in a meeting. When he heard it was the FBI Director and that it was urgent, he immediately took her call.

"Bill," said Watson, "I don't have time to give you all the details (she figured now wasn't a good time to educate the mayor on time travel) but all I have to tell you is that it's a matter of urgent national security. You need to put a stop work order on the construction site on corner of 119th and First Avenue. I'll fill you in on the details later."

"I don't know if I have the legal authority to do that Madam Director. The construction unions won't like that a bit, and because part of the plan includes a new school, I'll get heat from the teachers' union too. I'll have to consult with counsel."

Watson fantasized about putting a bullet through the phone.

"Bill, just do it. Just fucking do it. If you get yelled at by the City Council you'll be able to say that it was a direct request from the FBI based on national security. I'll back you up all the way. Do it, Bill. Do it now."

The mayor had been getting a lot of heat in the press for wrong-headed decisions. He was also under constant pressure from labor unions, the people who funded his election campaign. He could just picture the headlines. "Mayor Stops Construction Project Without Court Order." He also pondered that as mayor of New York City, he didn't take orders from the FBI.

"I'm sorry, Madam Director, but I have to go through proper channels."

"You will have a court order shortly," said Watson through clenched teeth, "verbal followed by email and physical papers. If you don't comply with the order I will personally escort you to prison."

Watson called Lysle Buchanan, senior Federal District Court Judge for the Southern District of New York. Watson was friends with the judge, having sat on the Southern District court herself five years ago. His clerk told her that the judge was presiding over a murder trial.

"The judge knows me. I'm the Director of the FBI and this is a matter of national security. Barge into that courtroom and tell him I need to talk to him NOW."

Judge Buchanan was on the phone in less than half a minute.

"Sarah, my old friend, good to hear from you," said Judge Buchanan. "How's your exciting new job going?"

"Lysle," said Watson, "I don't have a lot of time. I need a stop work order for a construction project on the East Side. If the construction continues it can result in the loss of thousands of lives from a terrorist attack. I can't give you a lot of details, but I need that order now."

Well," said the judge, "if the FBI Director tells me she needs a piece of paper, who am I to doubt her. Just give me the management and location details and I'll draft an order immediately. I'll personally call the company president and give him a verbal order and tell him the paperwork will be arriving shortly."

"God bless you, Lysle. Can I convince you to run for mayor of New York City?"

"What?"

"Long story. Thanks again, Lysle."

Back at the site, the construction foreman was digging in his heels. We could see a crane approaching the wormhole spot.

"Bennie," I said, "do something. Just do something. Do you have your badge?"

Bennie reentered the site as the foreman approached him, looking pissed. Bennie flashed his NYPD badge and walked toward him. He looked at the guy's name badge.

"Mr. Guarino," Ben said, "I'm detective Ben Weinberg of the NYPD. What's your first name?"

"Sal."

"Sal, you haven't committed a crime, but I'm telling you that this site involves national security. As you know, the criminal law isn't what it was a couple of years ago, so let me be perfectly clear, Sal. If you work on this section I will place you under arrest, and we'll figure out a charge later. Now I don't want to do that, Sal, and you don't want me to do that. I'm just asking you to slow down. We should have a court order shortly. Meantime, I don't think your project is going to collapse if you don't work on this part of the site today. What'll it be, Sal?"

"Do I have a choice?" said Guarino.

"No, you don't. So why don't you and your guys enjoy a break."

Within 45 minutes a gray car pulled up to the curb. A young man in a business suit got out and yelled to no one in particular, "I'm from Federal Judge Buchanan's office and I have a temporary restraining order to cease work on this site."

When you go from despair to elation in an hour, it plays with your emotions. We all hugged like a bunch of kids whose team just won the World Series. We won much more than that.

CHAPTER 36

You can call me Philip Murphy, but I prefer you call me Mohammed Islam, my true name. As Philip Murphy, I'm an American naval officer and I'm in charge of the weapons department on the aircraft carrier *USS George Washington.* As Mohammed Islam, I am a jihadi, a weapon in the arsenal of Allah.

I guess that sounds strange. Not many American naval officers call themselves by the proud title of jihadi, a man who struggles for the justice of Allah. And strange as it may sound, it would even sound stranger to the people I work with and who work for me. My second identity, the one known as Philip Murphy, is very good at playing his role. It's been a role I've played for over twenty years. Soon, Allah be willing, I can give up that role and be the true me, Mohammed Islam.

Twenty years ago I was an 18-year-old high school kid. Twenty years ago I couldn't imagine being the man I am today. Twenty years ago I had no idea what Islam was all about.

A man named Ayham Abboud changed all that. In 1994 I took a school trip to Riyadh, Saudi Arabia. Sheik Abboud was my mentor, as well as the counselor of four other kids on the trip. Our journey was arranged and sponsored by a group called *The Center for Open-Minded Youth,* funded by our host country Saudi Arabia. Sheik Abboud was about 25 and spoke English with a perfect American accent, which I guess should be expected because he's American.

I had no idea what to expect, but the idea of a vacation in an exotic place that my parents didn't have to pay for sounded great. I was what you would call a typical American teenager, and my main goals in life were forbidden pleasures, especially sex, which my Roman Catholic religion was especially touchy about. I had decent grades, but nothing great. I managed to get into George Washington University, after which I went to Officers Candidate School and became a commissioned officer in the United States Navy. Ayham Abboud had a lot to do with my going to OCS after college, as I'll explain shortly.

So there I was, a typical horny American teenager, in a strange land that seemed like a movie set. Sheik Abboud gathered me and my friends Joe Monahan, Ralph Martin, Fred Peyton, and George Quentin, and slowly began to change our lives.

We all stayed in the same dormitory, just the five of us and Sheik Abboud in a private room. Every day began with prayers, which we all thought strange. None of us were deeply religious, so we figured it wasn't any big deal. We knelt on rugs and prayed simple but uplifting prayers that the Sheik gave to us. He then began to lecture us on the mysteries and beauty of his faith, Islam. Abboud's words and our prayers began to change our thinking, in ways I can't remember, but in a way that was irreversible. After a month we had all converted to Islam, not as a fluke thing to do, but as a deep commitment from the heart. My life had changed in four weeks.

Sheik Abboud lectured us on commitment, especially to our newfound religion, and on the traits of dedication and discipline. He told us that we were warriors in the army of Islam, and that Allah had chosen us to perform a special mission, a mission that would not take place for years. The Sheik counseled me to become a commissioned officer in the United States Navy, a first step in a plan that would be revealed in time. Over the years we would meet periodically with Sheik Abboud as he helped us focus on our journey to come.

Our sacred mission, *my* sacred mission, is now only weeks away. I will tear at the hearts of the infidels, and begin the march to a new and glorious caliphate in America.

CHAPTER 37

That evening we all had dinner at Patsy's, a great Italian Restaurant on 57th Street. I asked the host to seat us where we'd have the most privacy. I gave him a generous tip with Ben's money.

"We're about to take a strange trip, a trip not to a different place but to a different time," I said. "I promise you it will feel weird. I know, I've been there. Let's talk about our journey and make some detailed plans for our arrival in 2015. We'll be in the same place we left, the site on 119th and First Avenue. It will look very different, a weed choked vacant lot with no construction going on. Based on my past experience, I have no idea what the weather will be, or even what day or month we'll land in. After we go through the wormhole, we'll take a flight to Norfolk, Virginia where the *Abraham Lincoln* is home ported. I'll get you guys booked into the Marriott near the base. Ashley and I have an apartment nearby, and we can use it as a base of operations."

"I have a practical question," said Wally. "Will any of our credit cards work?"

"No," I said, "but Ashley has all sorts of contacts so we'll arrange for new identities. Meanwhile, don't worry about money."

"That's right," said Bennie. "Celebrity Jack is loaded."

"You're rich?" said Janice.

"I make a living."

"Once we get to Norfolk I'll meet with Ashley. Then we'll all regroup and plan how to stop the Thanksgiving Attacks. As a Navy captain, Ashley will be in charge because it's a Navy matter. But I'm sure we'll have to enlist some political firepower just like we did with the FBI and CIA here in 2017. It shouldn't be a problem. Ashley and I have a lot of credibility on the subject of time travel. My guess is that the FBI or CIA will take over and we'll all be deputized again."

"So, my friends," I said, "tomorrow we do the impossible."

Chapter 38

We arrived at the wormhole site at 7 AM on July 22, a bright morning with low humidity. Because time travel is best done in privacy, we wanted to be early to avoid people. FBI Director Watson arranged for us each to have letters of authorization to be on the construction site. We stood as a group with our backs to the street. I would go first, then, by a coin flip, Wally, then Janice, followed by Bennie.

I stepped across the grate. I felt slightly nauseous, took a deep breath, then realized I had made the trip. It's a feeling I'll never get used to and I hope I won't have the opportunity again. I turned to welcome my friends. They appeared one by one, and as each came through the portal, I reached out to help them get steady. When I reached for Janice's arm she hugged me. They each had the same feeling as me, nausea and dizziness, and an overwhelming feeling of disbelief. The field was nothing like the one we left. Now it was just a vacant lot covered with weeds. When we left 2017, the temperature was 75 degrees and the sky was sunny. Now it was overcast and chilly. I pointed to the neon sign on the building.

11 AM October 1, 2015. The temperature was 48 degrees.

I thought I'd pass out. I had been gone for three months. The Thanksgiving Attacks are just eight weeks away. Obviously the time differential works different in the future than it does in the past. Time went faster, and our mission was now an emergency.

Ben, Janice and Wally just stood shivering and stared at our surroundings silently.

"There was a skyscraper right there when we left 2017," said Bennie, pointing east.

We noticed that there were very few cops around. One walked by, smiled and said hello. He didn't ask for our papers.

I took my cell phone out of my pocket, and was happy to find that my account was current, one of the nice things about electronic auto pay. I called my secretary at the *Washington Times* and told her to book us a flight from New York to Norfolk. She started to ask where the hell I'd been, that everybody had been freaking out over my disappearance. I told her I'd fill her in later. She called our well-trained travel department and phoned back within five minutes to tell me that our flight would leave from JFK at 2 PM.

Next, I called Ashley. It's been three months. I can't believe it.

"Jack, Honey, just talk, just let me hear your voice," Ashley said. "Where are you?"

"I'm catching a 2 PM flight from JFK to Norfolk. Arrival time is 2:53."

"Next question," said Ashley. "Where have you been?"

"Two years away," I said. "Yup, it happened again. Long story, Hon, a long and weird story. I'll meet you at the ship."

"No," Ashley said. "Meet me at the apartment. I want you all to myself."

I could tell she was fighting back tears. Ashley has a full range of emotions just like anybody, but as a military leader she's used to keeping her feelings in check. She'll let go when we see each other.

We took a cab to JFK and arrived at 12:15 PM. Next stop, Norfolk.

CHAPTER 39

We arrived in Norfolk right on time at 2:53. The travel office at the *Times* had booked three rooms at the Marriott near the Navy base. Ben, Janice, and Wally got out of the cab, and I continued on to meet Ashley at our apartment.

I lost my key somewhere in 2017, so I rang the doorbell. Ashley almost tackled me as she opened the door. We held each other and didn't speak, hugging like we didn't want to risk drifting away. Finally, Ashley started to talk, but broke down crying.

It wasn't the time we were apart that gripped us, it was the uncertainty of whether we'd ever see each other again. After three months, Ashley must have tried to avoid thinking that I'd be missing forever. And after only three weeks in 2017, I constantly struggled with the uncertainty of being on the other side of a wormhole.

Ashley held my face in her hands and stared into my eyes. Ashley has the most expressive eyes of any woman I'd ever known. She was giving me what everybody calls an *Ashley Patterson Eye Job*.

"When you went missing," said Ashley, as she put her arms around my neck, "I assumed it was a time trip, given that certain weird part of your profile Mr. Time Magnet. But as the days, weeks and months went by I started to feel something I never felt before – despair. But now you're here in my arms where you belong."

"Have I mentioned that I love you," I said.

"It's been a while," Ashley said, "but it sounds great to hear it."

"Okay, Honey," Ashley said, reluctantly changing the subject, "I've got to know what happened, but first I have to know this. I'm not exactly unfamiliar with time travel. So why didn't you just step back on the wormhole right after you came through to the other side? From everything you've ever said or written about time travel, that's the way to come back."

"If I did that, you and I would have eight weeks to live."

Ashley stared, wide eyed.

"I need to sit down," said Ashley. "Here, sit next to me. I don't want you out of my sight."

"Okay, Sweetheart, here it is from the top. History, the history that I learned in my three weeks in 2017, tells us that on Thanksgiving Day, 2015—two months from now—five American carriers will be attacked with suitcase nuclear bombs. One of those ships will be the *Abraham Lincoln.* As you know, because you've already invited me, I'll be with you on the ship. There will be no survivors, including you and me. In all, about 26,000 people will die on all of the ships. The other carriers were the *Roosevelt*, the *Truman*, the *Vinson*, and the *George Washington.* The event became known as the Thanksgiving Attacks, the greatest terrorist spectacular in history."

Ashley began to perspire. She fell back against the couch, squeezing my hand all the time, staring at me, not saying anything.

"So what I've been up to for the last three weeks, or three months of 2015 time, is acting like a detective. My sole objective was to gather objective evidence that I could bring back with me so I could blow the whistle, and get people to hear it. Now I've got the evidence, and I've only got eight weeks to stop the attacks."

"Dear God" Said Ashley, "Dear God Almighty. Jack, tell me about the evidence."

"We have conclusive evidence that the attackers, the people who set the bombs, were the weapons officers on the five carriers, including Joe Monahan on the *Lincoln.*"

"Joe Monahan is a murdering terrorist?" Ashley asked, almost screaming.

"Yes," I said, "He and the others were radicalized as teenagers at an indoctrination camp in Saudi Arabia. They have been deep moles for over twenty years. I'll fill in details later, but for right now, let me ask you a question, has Monahan ordered a special air conditioning unit for the ship's magazine?"

"Holy shit," Ashley shouted. "Yes, yes he has. And I know of at least one other ship that ordered an air conditioner for the magazine. Ike Bollinger of the *Vinson* told me about it. Neither of us knew what to make of it. What are the air conditioners all about?"

"Bomb holders," I said.

Ashley got off the couch, went over to the wet bar and splashed cold water on her face. She sat back down next to me and breathed deeply.

"God knows," Ashley said, "I've handled some heavy duty stuff before, but nothing like this."

"Where are we in the operation, Jack, what's our status and what's the plan?"

"Tomorrow morning you're going to meet three people who were at my side during the whole investigation. All three of them came with me through the wormhole. We've even given ourselves a name, *The Thanksgiving Gang*. Their names are, Bennie Weinberg who you know very well, a guy named Wally Burton from *The New York Times,* and Janice Monahan, Joe Monahan's wife.

"Joe Monahan's wife?" Ashley gasped.

"Yes, and she's not his biggest fan."

"Okay," said Ashley, "I've got a million questions to ask, but it's probably best for you to just fill me in on the details along with the others. You know, I expected that when I finally saw you I'd feel nothing but relief. Now I feel numb. Let me take a few deep breaths and calm down."

Ashley is a practitioner of deep breathing meditation, and she's gotten me into it as well. It's especially useful when you're under stress, and I'm afraid that's exactly what I've given Ashley, a lot of stress. After a couple of minutes of deep breathing, which I joined her in, we both felt better.

"You look exhausted, Honey," Ashley said after her deep breathing routine. "Why don't you take a shower and relax."

She smiled and stroked my face. "I'll even help you."

Ashley and I have some catching up to do.

* * *

"When you make admiral are we still going to carry on like this?" I asked.

"Twice as much," Ashley said.

CHAPTER 40

The next morning Ashley called the ship and told Mike Cummings, her new executive office, to cover for her.

Bennie, Janice, and Wally showed up promptly at 8:30.

Janice shook Ashley's hand and said, "I met you once at the officer's club with Joe. You and Jack had just gotten married. Jack's a lucky man and you're a lucky woman. Maybe you guys can introduce me to an eligible bachelor who isn't a treasonous murderer."

"I'll work on it, Janice," said Ashley as she gave her a hug.

"Bennie," Ashley said, "I haven't seen you since the Naval Board of Inquiry after the *California* incident. Jack tells me that you're now an official time tripper. Welcome back to 2015."

"I can't tell you how good it is to see you, Ashley," said Ben as he grasped both of Ashley's hands. "I guess Jack told you that everybody thought you and Jack were dead. Let's make sure that doesn't happen."

We had just begun to eat the bagels I ordered when the doorbell rang. As Ashley went to the door, I noticed that she reached under her sweater and drew her gun. She held it discretely behind her. We could all hear the man at the door say, "I'm Special Agent Gamal Akhbar of the CIA. May I come in?"

"Buster," the four of us shouted. Ashley looked at us, then at the man. We surrounded Buster like a bunch of high school kids welcoming their coach.

"We call agent Akhbar, Buster," I explained to Ashley. "He was our team leader."

"He *is* your team leader, not *was*," Buster corrected me. "Did you really think the Agency would leave this mission to a bunch of amateurs?"

"How the hell did you get here?" asked Wally.

"Simple," said Buster," I watched you all disappear into the wormhole and I followed you. When I passed through the portal and saw the month and year we're in, I realized that we have an emergency, not just a mission. The attacks are only a few weeks away. The CIA Director went right to the White House and got an executive order putting the wormhole site off limits until the order is rescinded. The wormhole is there, if we need it."

"Captain," Buster turned to Ashley, "I apologize if I seem to be taking over, but it's my assignment."

"Please, Buster, if I may call you that," Ashley said, "I think we all know that we need a professional to pull this off. Just tell us what you need."

"Yes, please call me Buster. May I call you Ashley?"

"Of course."

Buster went out to his rented car to retrieve something. He came back with a laptop, a projector, an easel, and a flipchart. Besides having balls of brass, Buster is a master planner.

"Okay," Buster said, "here's where we are, and here's where we want to go. Our working theory is that the nuclear devices were planted in special air conditioning units that were or will be placed in the ships' magazines. As an a/c engineer, Janice has been invaluable. Now, Ashley, let me ask you, is Monahan still on the *Lincoln?*"

"Yes, he is. About the air conditioner, an alarm went off in my head when he requested it. I met with my friend Ike Bollinger, captain of the *Carl Vinson*. His weapons officer asked for the same thing on that ship. I didn't go any further with it, just assuming that Monahan, like the guy on the *Vinson,* was being a diligent officer. Bollinger thought the same thing. I have no idea about the other ships, but it should be easy to find out. I can simply call each of the captains and ask if they had a requisition for a special a/c unit for the magazine."

"Do you know if the air conditioner has been delivered to the *Lincoln* yet?" Buster asked.

"No, I don't," Ashley said. "I'll find out right now."

She called Commander Mike Cummings, her executive officer. "Mike, I need you to check on something for me, and I need you to do it quietly. Not a word to anyone, especially Joe Monahan. I want you to check our requisition requests and find out if that air conditioner that Monahan wanted has been delivered. It's all on the computer so you can just do a search."

Janice waved her hand.

"Hold on Mike," Ashley said.

"Tell him it's a Tomlinson Model 2000," Janice said. "It may help his search."

"Mike, It's a Tomlinson Model 2000. Remember not a word to anybody. I'll explain when I see you."

Buster hooked up his laptop to the projector and flashed a PowerPoint display on the wall. Each theory was listed in sequence, from the weapons officers as suspects to the air conditioners as bomb holders.

"The people at Langley think the air conditioners are just receptacles to hold the bombs. The thinking is that they're suitcase bombs and will be put in the units after they're delivered.

The phone rang. It was Mike Cummings for Ashley.

"No captain," said Cummings, "no air conditioning units have been delivered to the ship, but I did find the purchase order."

"Thanks, Mike," said Ashley, "I'll talk to you later."

"I'll take that as good news," said Buster. "It will make it easier to intercept them before delivery. We can also contact the Tomlinson Company to find out when they're due to be shipped."

"But understand that this is now an emergency. Trevor McMartin's kidnapping told us something, something big. It told us that somebody was on to us, somebody who didn't want McMartin to give us photos of the weapons officers."

"But that was in 2017," Janice said. "Can't we assume that any conspirators in this year don't know about our meeting with Trevor, not to mention our plan?"

"That's all we can hope for," said Buster. "But we also know that this conspiracy is a lot bigger than five guys. It seems simple. We arrest the five and we're done. But it's not that simple. First, what the hell do we arrest them for? Jack has some undated pictures placing these men in various places in the Middle East. So what? Can you imagine me presenting a photo of a guy in front of a Middle Eastern bank and saying to a judge, 'Well obviously he's a bad guy, judge, may I please have a warrant for his arrest?' And if we wait until one of them commits a crime, and carrying a suitcase nuke aboard a Navy ship would qualify, how the hell do we know who makes the delivery? And further, if we wait for whoever delivers the bombs to act, how do we know that it can't be detonated on the spot? They'd achieve the same result, just a different location."

"So why don't we just kill the bastards?" asked Janice, our born-again warrior. Wow, this woman really has anger issues about her husband.

"Well," said Buster, "I'm not saying the Agency would condone such an action without legal backup, but either way it wouldn't solve the problem. It would just replace one problem with another, maybe even a bigger one. We don't have any idea where the weapons are. If we take out the five known bad boys, whoever has the bombs may just detonate them in the middle of large cities. The Thanksgiving Attacks would simply move from sea to land. If we had time, which we don't, we could launch a full-scale investigation of the five and eventually we'd locate the weapons. Today's October 2. Eight weeks from now hell opens up. Bottom line, folks, we've got to find the goddam bombs."

"What about enhanced interrogation?" said Bennie. "I've always had mixed feelings about water boarding, but with 26,000 lives on the line, not to mention Ashley and Jack here, it starts to look like the morally correct thing to do."

"Okay, Jack Bauer," said Buster, referring to America's favorite terror stopper. "Forget the moral issue. If I thought it would solve the problem, I'd blow their fucking heads off right now. But if we apprehend them and take them out of action while we politely inter-rogate them, what about the bad guys they communicate with, the bad guys who actually have the bombs. They'd simply go to Plan B, and I don't think we'd like Plan B."

"We have to think of this as a military operation," said Ashley. "Beginning now, and I mean right now, we place radiological detec-tion devices at all of the entrances to every ship. I see this as a SEAL operation. Once we detect that a person is carrying a nuke, two or three SEALs move in and separate the device from the person, before he or she has a chance to detonate it. I'm sure the firing mechanism isn't a hair trigger or else they'd have to worry about the bomb going off in a fender bender. No, I've read articles about suitcase nukes. It takes some doing to arm one of these things."

"Captain Ashley, "said Buster, "you make a damn good point. If we can't pull off any other plan, we will be left with the only option to detect, grab, and neutralize. Just remember, we're dealing with nuclear weapons. The less violent the plan the better."

"So Buster," I said, "what do you think? Ashley's plan looks like the only possible last minute scenario. What happens between now and then?"

"Surveillance," said Buster, "the tightest and fastest surveillance this country's ever pulled off. We need drones and satellites tracking the Atomic Five every time they're outdoors. We need phone taps. We need GPS plants on their vehicles and their persons. If one hops a cab, the cab gets a GPS tracker. We need to track every waking moment in the lives of these killers. I'm betting that as the time gets closer, their planning activities will pick up the pace. What worries me is that the time for these guys to move around between the ships and the bomb locations may have passed. They may be at an advanced stage of their mission which calls for them to stay put."

CHAPTER 41

Sheik Abbas Haddad sat in the back of a Toyota Land Cruiser driven by his assistant Amjad Boulos. The October sun was setting, casting a sad golden glow across the buildings of Detroit as the car drove through the once prosperous streets. Haddad loved the setting sun and its way of making even ugly things beautiful.

Haddad has been a high official in al-Qaeda for two years, although his status has been hidden from the public, especially the Western press. He was picked for the job because of his intelligence, courage, and fanatical devotion to the outer reaches of jihad. His superiors know that Haddad wants the West do die, and that he wants to be the one to kill it.

The car pulled into the parking lot of an abandoned Chrysler factory. According to the procedures he devised, Haddad rode in a different car on each visit. Also, according to his plans, he was driven to a back entrance that couldn't be seen from the street.

The car's approach was seen from inside the building, as was the approach of any vehicle. As Haddad approached the door it opened. A man with an AK-47 slung over his shoulder bowed.

"Peace be upon you, Sheik Haddad," the man with the gun said.

The room was cavernous, about the size of a football field. In the center was a structure 100 feet by 200 feet made of standard sheet rock walls. Haddad walked through the door of the structure and the six men present bowed.

"I wish to speak to Ali Hakimi alone," Haddad said. The five others left the room.

"I have an important question to ask you, Ali," Haddad said. "Have you seen or heard from Sheik Ayham Abboud?"

"No, my Sheik. I haven't seen him in weeks. I was about to ask you the same question."

"As you know, Ali, Sheik Abboud is critical to our operation. He is the man who converted our Navy brothers 20 years ago, and introduced them to their sacred mission. I fear for his safety. If you hear from him or from anyone who knows his whereabouts let me know immediately."

"Tell me my brother Ali," said Haddad, changing the subject, "are we ready to bring the fires of hell to the infidels?"

"We will be ready to strike in two weeks, my Sheik," said Haddad.

The two men walked over to a long table. Five suitcases were set on top of the table, each measuring 8 in. by 16 in. by 24 in. Every suitcase weighed just over 50 pounds. Inside each was the mechanism of a one kiloton nuclear bomb. The weapons had been purchased for $5 Million American dollars from a Vladimir Trushenko, a Russian bomb expert in charge of security for the weapons. After the transaction had been completed, Trushenko was murdered and the money reclaimed.

"They will be delivered by our brothers, the weapons officers," said Haddad. "Because they each have Top Secret security clearances, we don't anticipate a problem with the deliveries."

"And what about the arming procedure, Ali?" asked Haddad.

"Each of the men has been trained and retrained on arming the devices. They're scheduled to return here twice before the delivery date to make sure everything is coordinated perfectly. The bombs will be armed the morning of the detonations. As you ordered, each of the five bombs will detonate exactly one minute after the one before it, beginning at 3 PM Eastern Time. If I may be so bold, sir, your idea of spacing the explosions is brilliant. It will totally confuse the infidels' news networks. They will gather information on one explosion and then be confronted with the following one. They won't know that we have set five weapons, so the American government will be like a pack of insane jackals trying to anticipate what will happen next."

"And the date of delivery?" asked Haddad.

"They will be delivered on November 25, the day before the infidel Thanksgiving, the day before we change their world."

"May Allah bless you for your work, Ali."

Chapter 42

"Captain," said Buster, "you have a lot of influence and we're going to need every bit of it. Nobody's going to believe a spook from the future like me. As a CIA agent, I can get surveillance orders, but as soon as we have a few shreds of evidence, we'll need to go upstairs for authority to make arrests. I suggest that you contact the Chief of Naval Intelligence. For now, just tell him that you have credible evidence that there may be plots against some of our ships. You should take Jack with you. The both of you have a lot of credibility. If we can get enough evidence from surveillance of the Atomic Five, you won't even have to discuss time travel with the CNI, just enough for him to detain them."

"When will the drones and satellites start looking?" asked Janice.

"They've started already. They don't call me Buster for nothing."

CHAPTER 43

Lieutenant Commander George Quentin, (Jazeer Mohammed) Weapons Officer *USS Harry S. Truman*, walked down the gangplank to a waiting cab which would take him to the airport. He was on four days' leave, enough time for him to take care of business in Detroit. The *Truman* was docked in San Diego.

An overhead helicopter drone tracked him to the airport where one of Buster's operatives took note of his flight and destination. The operative then contacted Buster who alerted his man in Detroit. When the plane landed, another drone picked up Quentin's trail, following the cab from the airport to the old Chrysler plant. It circled overhead taking photos of Quentin as he entered the building and relaying the photos to CIA headquarters where Buster had a top secret team at work. His operative called Buster to tell him about Quentin.

"Fucking bullseye," said Buster. "Well, maybe it's a bullseye. It's possible Quentin may just like to enjoy vacation time at an abandoned factory in Detroit."

The drone also tracked Quentin's movements from Detroit back to the *USS Truman* in San Diego.

One of Buster's operatives called him from Mayport, Florida where the *USS Theodore Roosevelt* was docked. He told Buster that the drone had just picked up Lieutenant Commander Frederick Peyton (Lashkar Islamiyah).

"I'm guessing he's going to spend some leave time in beautiful downtown Detroit," said Buster. "Keep me posted."

CHAPTER 44

My name is Joseph Monahan. I'm 39 years old and a lieutenant commander in the United States Navy. My current assignment is weapons officer on the *USS Abraham Lincoln*, a job I've planned on landing for a long time.

Ever since I was 18 years old, my life has had one mission, to strike at the heart of the heathen culture known as America. I was a high school senior when I took a trip to Riyadh, Saudi Arabia, sponsored by *The Center for Open-Minded Youth*. There I met four other high school students from the States. Together we began a journey that will soon end in destruction.

I converted to Islam by the fourth week of my stay in Saudi Arabia, as did my friends. We learned the joy of the true religion, the thrill of serving Allah, and the beauty of reading the Quran. Our spiritual leader was a young man named Ayham Abboud, who is still our leader to this day. Beside the wonders of Islam, Sheik Abboud taught us the importance of discipline and the need for secrecy. I never told my parents of my conversion, an event that occurred over 20 years ago. I went through the motions of a typical young American. They were proud when I was accepted to the Naval Reserve Officer Training Corps at the University of Michigan.

My other self appears to be a proud, diligent, and patriotic naval officer for all these years. But that's my other self, the self named Joseph Monahan. My true self, the person who I really am is Abu Hussein, a fighter in the cause of justice. That's what I've been told repeatedly over the past 20 years. Yes, I'm a jihadi, a terrorist.

I married a beautiful woman, Janice, and she is as ignorant of my Muslim self as are my parents. We've become distant recently, almost estranged. Over the years I've criticized her for the clothing she wears in public, the music she listens to, and the TV shows she watches. I think my regular carping has driven her away from me emotionally. I'm not sure I can blame her.

I miss Janice, the old Janice, the brilliant fun-loving beauty who I married, the woman who I drove away.

But none of that matters. In a few weeks my brothers and I will become the fist of Allah, and the infidels will cringe as we change their world. I will soon detonate a bomb that will kill the entire crew of the USS *Abraham Lincoln*, along with some civilians. Along with my fellow officers we will slaughter about 26,000 people all together. But that's okay because we call them heathens, barbarians, infidels. Yes, that's what we call them, and how we will think of them when we kill them. But if they're barbarians, what am I?

My mission is supposed to bring me joy, joy in the glory to come. I'm supposed to feel happy about setting a timer and killing thousands of people, husbands and wives, sisters and brothers. Many of them are friends of mine, friends of a man they thought they could trust, friends of a guy who's about to end their lives. I wonder how many orphans I'll make in a moment's time.

I don't feel joy, I feel confusion. I feel doubt.

CHAPTER 45

Over the next five days the drones and satellites tracked each of the other officers of the Atomic Five going to the same building in Detroit.

Buster had a team member at Langley research everything about the old Chrysler plant. It had been purchased in 2013 for $3 Million in cash by a company in Yemen. With over 60,000 square feet of floor space, the building could be used for any number of purposes. Large cargo doors are located on each of the four sides. The roof is flat, supported by steel girders for protection against heavy Michigan snowstorms. The entire lot surrounding the building is illuminated by floodlights. Security cameras are mounted every 100 feet, and a 50-foot perimeter surrounds the building, serving the function of a moat around a Medieval castle. No one can approach the structure without being detected.

Philip Oliver, one of the team members assigned to study the building, looked at satellite images of the roof. He also studied the original construction plans for the structure which were obtained from the engineering firm that designed it. The ventilation pipes from the original construction were still in place. Inside the building the vent pipes have openings about 20 feet off the floor. Oliver was trying to find a way to insert a camera into one or more of the vent pipes. He came up with a solution: a robot placed on the roof by a drone.

Oliver had found a way into the building.

CHAPTER 46

"Peace be with you, Commander Monahan," said Abbas Haddad, "although I prefer to call you Abu Hussein. Please have a seat."

Monahan sat on a straight back chair in the corner of Haddad's spare apartment in downtown Detroit. Haddad's wife, wearing a full burqa, served tea.

"I was expecting to meet with Ayham Abboud, sir," said Monahan. "I haven't seen him in a long while. My brother officers and I hold Sheik Abboud in the highest regard. He is the man who set us on the path to righteousness so many years ago."

"I have no idea of the whereabouts of Sheik Abboud," said Haddad. "He has been a critical part of our planning for this glorious mission. Nobody has heard from him in weeks. But we can proceed without him, as we must. I am now blessed with the leadership of this operation. As you well know, Abu, of all of our brother naval officers, your role is the most crucial. You have knowledge of details that the others don't. After this plan is carried out, you will be known as Sheik Abu Hussein, the former Joseph Monahan."

"You and your brother naval officers from the other ships will soon rewrite the history of Islam," said Haddad. Your courage and religious devotion will help us to bring forth a new caliphate in this heathen land. The world will soon know that the holy march of

Islam cannot be stopped. While the American pigs are stuffing their mouths with food, we will give them a new meaning of Thanksgiving Day. When the sun sets on that day, a new world shall have begun, a world that knows the wrath of Allah. Let us now discuss the steps that will be taken."

"Our plans are in order Sheik Haddad," said Monahan, "I have just come from our factory two miles from here. Our brothers have performed their bomb preparation tasks brilliantly. I see nothing that can interfere with the plan. As you say, the history of Islam will soon change."

"What about your wife, I believe Janice is her name. She suspects nothing?"

"Nothing at all, Sheik Haddad. I have kept my routine the same, except for the trips to Detroit. I told her that I was going to San Diego for a series of special training assignments."

"As for the details of the plan," said Haddad, "the weapons will be transported by vans on the afternoon of November 25, the day before Thanksgiving. Each of you will be alerted when the van approaches your ship. You will meet the van at the gate and carry the suitcase aboard. Once you have the weapon aboard and inserted into the air conditioner, you will set the timer to exactly 3 PM. Your brothers will set their timers in one-minute intervals after that. Just before the ship sails, you will fake the illness you have trained for and you will be taken ashore. I know that you do not fear to die for Islam, but we need your talents for the future. Your brother officers will each have a different way of missing their ship's sailing time. You will all be taken to different Muslim countries when the time is right."

"What is it Abu?" said Haddad. "You seem troubled, distracted, almost sad. Are you feeling alright?"

"It's nothing, my sheik," Monahan said. "The pressure of these past few weeks is intense."

CHAPTER 47

Buster, as usual, had a good idea. Rather than meet at our apartment, we needed a more secure location. The team gathered at a nondescript block building on the Navy base that serves from time to time as a technical school. The facility has four rooms, including two bathrooms, a kitchen, and a large classroom where we'll meet. The entrance is guarded by two armed Marines.

Besides the usual Thanksgiving Gang consisting of me, Buster, Janice, Bennie, Wally, and now Ashley, Vice Admiral Jerome Bettenhurst, the commander of Naval Intelligence, was with us. Admiral Bettenhurst was sent directly by the Chief of Naval Operations. Buster introduced us all to Bettenhurst. After a short introductory chat I was amazed how much Bettenhurst was up to speed on the entire operation. He was even ahead of us.

"I have some great news," Bettenhurst said. "We had a drone helicopter place a small camera- equipped robot on the roof of the Detroit factory. The robot travelled down a vent pipe and found an opening to take pictures. Here are the photos."

On the screen in front of us was the inside of the bomb factory itself, including a clear shot of a long table with five open suitcases, one of which was tilted on its side.

"I showed this picture to an expert at the CIA," said Bettenhurst. "He knows everything about suitcase nukes. He said that the device in the picture is definitely a nuclear weapon. He showed us in detail why he knew it was a bomb, showing us the wiring, the detonator and the timing device. I'll let my favorite spook Buster here bring us all up to the minute on where we are."

"Correct me if I'm wrong, Admiral," said Buster, "But I think we have enough for a raid and arrests. Am I on target?"

"You are, indeed, Buster. I had a group from the Justice Department look over my shoulder on this. They weren't let in on all the details, just the legal necessities. Right now we can arrest the people that you folks have referred to as the Atomic Five. We can also raid the Detroit building and confiscate the bombs. That second part won't be easy, so it will be a Navy SEAL operation. We don't want to blow up what's left of Detroit."

"Today is October 10th," said Ashley. "When will this happen?"

"Five days from now," said Bettenhurst. "The SEALs need time to prepare. We'll keep satellite and drone surveillance on the building to make sure the bombs aren't moved. The entire combined operation has been assigned the code Tango Delta, short for Thanksgiving Day."

"Who's going to arrest the Atomic Five?" asked Bennie.

"That will be handled by SEALs. I was going to assign the task to agents from Naval Intelligence, but it could get rough, and SEALs are good at rough."

"So I don't get to shoot my scumbag husband," Janice observed.

We all cracked up. Janice has a unique way of relieving tension.

But I'm getting nervous. At first this was a small operation with only a few people on board. Now it seems like half of Washington knows a piece of the puzzle.

CHAPTER 48

Two helicopters, each carrying 12 SEALs, landed in the parking lot of the old Chrysler plant. The SEALs' top objective was to secure the table with the bombs. They set plastique explosives and blew the doors off each of the four sides of the building. The men then rushed in and fired their carbines at anyone in sight. A man with an AK 47 stumbled from behind a cabinet and opened fire, knocking one SEAL to the floor. The bullets hit his flak jacket and he wasn't seriously injured. Another SEAL opened fire on the man, killing him instantly. Four SEALs ran to the bomb table, spun around and trained their weapons out toward anyone who approached. Four more SEALS dropped from the ceiling on ropes. The firing stopped after 45 seconds. The SEAL leader counted all of the enemy bodies and determined that the building was secure, except for one man.

Their second most important objective was to try to capture Abbas Haddad and take him alive if possible. But Haddad was nowhere to be seen. Apparently he worried enough about satellite and drone surveillance to have a look-alike slip in and out of the building. A man who resembled Haddad was tackled by two SEALs. They looked at their photos and then at the man. It wasn't him. Haddad had gotten away.

* * *

As soon as each of the arresting teams on the five ships got the word that the bomb factory was secure they moved in on the Atomic Five.

On the *USS Abraham Lincoln,* Joseph Monahan was surrounded and handcuffed as he emerged from his office. Monahan went quietly with his captors, his head turned down.

George Quentin had just assumed the quarterdeck watch on the *USS Harry S. Truman.*

"The good news is that you are relieved from your watch duty today," said the SEAL lieutenant. "The bad news is that you're under arrest for attempted murder and treason."

Ralph Martin, the weapons officer on the *USS Carl Vinson,* tried to run. He sprinted across the flight deck, intending to leap to the water, not expecting to live. He was tackled by the ship's Master at Arms who had been alerted to the operation.

Frederick Peyton was intercepted as he walked to the weapons department on the *USS Theodore Roosevelt.* As he was placed in handcuffs he cursed the SEAL lieutenant in Arabic, who returned the abuse in Spanish.

Philip Murphy had just completed lunch in the wardroom of the *USS George Washington.* As he walked down the companionway he was arrested and handcuffed by two Navy SEALS.

Operation Tango Delta was over in 25 minutes.

CHAPTER 49

It was 5:30 PM, October 16, 2015 and we had just gotten word that operation Tango Delta was a success.

"I think it's time for a party," I shouted.

Ashley called the Officers' Club and reserved a private room. Admiral Bettenhurst had to leave to get back to Washington where he'd debrief the Chief of Naval Operations. Just as well. The Thanksgiving Gang wanted the evening to ourselves.

"So, Jack, my amazing friend," said Bennie, "you've done it again. You changed history. You also saved your beautiful wife, not to mention yourself and about 26,000 people."

"A slight correction, Bennie," I said. "*We* changed history. I couldn't have pulled this off without you guys. You're the best friends any man could hope for." With that I abandoned my steely demeanor as a journalist and broke down crying. Ashley walked over and wrapped her arms around me.

"You're the best friends I could ever have too," said Ashley. "I had almost given this guy up for dead, and you brought him back to me." Then Ashley started to cry.

"Hey gang," said Janice. "This is supposed to be a celebration not a friggin' funeral. Let's stop crying and remember some of the funny parts about this whole operation."

"Funny parts?" said Buster. "What funny parts?"

"Give me some time, I'll think of something," said Janice.

"I think it was kind of funny the way Janice shot that guy in the restaurant in Yemen," said Wally. We all cracked up, except for Ashley.

"Janice shot a man in a restaurant and you think that's funny?" said Ashley.

"You hadda be there," said Wally.

We talked and reminisced till the wee hours of the morning when we all realized that we needed sleep. Bennie said he'd call a couple of cabs.

"There's a limo on the way for us," said Buster. "Hey, we CIA guys know how to spend taxpayer dollars."

As we waited for the limo Ashley and I just stared into each other's eyes. It's good to be alive.

Chapter 50

Abbas Haddad took a taxi to an industrial area of Denver, Colorado. The air was chilly and a light rain fell. He got out of the cab, waited for it to drive away, then turned and walked in the opposite direction. Keeping a lookout for any passersby, he ducked into a fence opening and walked up to an industrial warehouse. It looks just like the old Chrysler building in Detroit he thought. His approach to the building was detected from the inside and the door swung open without his having to knock. The inside of the building looked almost exactly like the one in Detroit only smaller. The same walled-off area was over to the right, and two men with AK 47s stood at its entrance. The walls were the same height and color. The table holding five nuclear suitcase bombs looked the same as the one in Detroit

"May peace be with you Sheik Haddad," said a man with a rifle slung around his shoulder. "Brother Hussein awaits you, sir."

Hussein Basara bounded out of his office adjacent to a large walled off area. He smiled at his old friend.

Haddad didn't smile back. He grabbed Basara by the shoulders, looked him in the eyes and said, "Are you ready to raise the fist of Allah against the infidels, my brother?"

About the Author

I'm the author of *The Gray Ship* (Coddington Press 2013), book one of *The Time Magnet* series. It's a story of time travel, romance, and a nuclear warship that finds itself in the Civil War. *The Thanksgiving Gang* is the sequel.

I have also published five nonfiction books: *Justice in America: How it Works—How it Fails.* (Coddington Press, 2011); *The APT Principle — The Business Plan That You Carry in Your Head.* (Coddington Press, 2012); *Boating Basics, the Boattalk Book of Boating Tips* (Coddington Press, 2013); *How to Create More Time* (Coddington Press, 2014). I'm a lawyer and a veteran of the United States Navy. I live in Long Island, New York with my wife Lynda.

WELCOME!

Welcome to *The Time Magnet Series*. The book you've just read, *The Thanksgiving Gang*, is Book Two of the series, the sequel to *The Gray Ship*. If you enjoyed reading *The Thanksgiving Gang,* you'll love *The Gray Ship*, the beginning of the saga.

You can find *The Gray Ship* on Kindle and paperback on amazon. com

I hope you enjoyed *The Thanksgiving Gang*. Please consider giving it a review on amazon.com.

Want to be updated on the next book in the series? Please copy this link to be added to my update list as well as a free subscription to my weekly blog on writing tips, *The Write Stuff*. http://www. morancom.com/

When you get to the site, just click on "Subscribe and get updates in the right hand column.

Made in the USA
San Bernardino, CA
06 November 2015